Glowbox

CB Cooper

Table of Contents

Chapter 1: Hurricane Force Winds

There are moments in the lives of every living thing that determine the rest of it. It can be obvious that a game-changer is in the works. Sometimes, it's impossible to distinguish blessings from curses! Either way, when you're reflecting later down the road, you're like, "Woah"! You never see it coming.

You will wake up expecting a normal, boring day, but before you know it, winds of change blow your life into a completely new direction. Hence the expression: You never can tell. You usually can't. Life happens fast.

It's hard to pinpoint exactly what road led to what path. Was there ever a path to start with? It all gets jumbled. Life is full of so many steps.

There are epic sagas that begin with a whisper's decibel. They take you through hurricane-force winds just to get back to shore. You can't tell if it's for better or for worse, maybe both. You may even end up on a different beach. These are the great ones, mine's no different.

Where does it start? Where does it end? One thing truly does lead to another. It's kind of like a merry-go-round.

My game took its most interesting when I had to use the Glowbox just to try and save my own butt on the spot. Nothing has been anything like normal since I had to jump through time. Rose, here I am with you now. I don't want my old normal back.

New love is so fresh and tender and soft. It seems to be composed almost entirely of explosions. It's mostly bursts of energy and compassion that have been stored deep down, waiting for the right conditions to ignite. That's what you've done for me.

A seed waiting to sprout just lays quietly in its place waiting to use the elements correctly to spring to life. That's what I feel like you've done to me sweetie. You sparked my birth or rebirth into existence. I was dormant until I met you.

I was bumbling around the sixties with no real sense of purpose. I knew I was where I wanted to be. That's all I could say about it. I was just kind of drifting along until that day on the beach when we met.

That's how I ended up on this broken-down Hubert Humphrey bench in Golden Gate Park. It's the summer of '68. I was born in 1983, darling. So, the appearance of the Glowbox was a crazy twist of fate for a little ole country boy.

Hippy-era San Francisco is a cool thing to witness. It's an especially peaceful place to stretch my legs out, having come up in the hectic Desert Storm/NWA era of America. Our country was at war for what seemed like my whole life. America was always at war with other countries, as well as the ones in the streets.

I got so used to the electronic entry methods of my day. I kept trying to push the unlock button on my car keys at the front door to the house. I thumb the top of these old metal keys, looking for the button now. It isn't there, of course.

This demonstrates how my instincts left from my past life in the future get confused in my conscious. It's a comical thing to me now, and I laugh at myself for doing it. I'll admit it took some getting used to. I don't mind it, though.

Time travel will really take a toll on you. Don't think jet lag's bad, ever, please. This world is amazing, from what I've seen. Do you like traveling?

Well try to grasp, readying yourself for a journey to a distant era. Imagine a whole different region of the planet. Now, in my case, it was a completely foreign time. The zap that stuff leaves on you must make jet lag feel like a little burp or hiccup.

This all started by accident. I was just being nosey and ogling a machine no one knew existed. Then my bosses show up unexpectedly. I tried to think fast and use the thing and ended up a traveling hobo of the clock and calendars. I can't get too comfortable when I don't belong at that age and time. Also, I worry myself to death, wondering if there's any way for them to track and find me.

Thank goodness I've found a home, a place to finish my days. I believe I'll pull off the grafting of myself into this beautiful melting pot of energies they call San Francisco. It's a nice change from North Michigan winters in the Upper Peninsula, that's for sure.

I've lived here for years now, peacefully too, I must add, which makes this a huge change of pace. It's also a welcome one at that. Vietnam is a crazy issue, but street violence is far less.

Let me take you on a walk through the Haight. Picture a beehive, a colorful, calm, but unstable beehive. These bees, though, are young, strong-minded folks, however, and don't just swarm any weak threat.

They save their energy for surgical strikes, the elite of the "Hippies" at least. The cool thing is they are like a beautiful, soft-hearted little army. So, of course, they have forces everywhere. This is much different than the pockets of resistance of the latter days, like Anonymous.

I was really into psychedelic rock in the 90s. So, this just seemed like a good spot to call my home. I was jamming out to Hendrix and Zepplin in the nineties. All my friends were obsessed with Nirvana and Soundgarden.

This is the place for me. I was not prepared for the magnetic force of the electricity in the air. It's not just in the air, though it's in the water, the earth, and Lord knows you can feel the fire! The Vietnam Conflict is intense.

You know that nervous tension you feel all around you downtown in rush hour traffic sometimes? Picture that times a million. Add to that the fact your friends are being forced off in droves to fight some war in a jungle. The jungle is also halfway across the globe.

The draft wasn't in existence when I was in service, but I was young as hell when I enlisted. I really sympathize with the young men being drafted these days. I feel like I'm sitting on a nuclear bomb. I know how it all turns out, so it's wild to feel all this excitement in the air.

I taught a stranger to use the Glowbox. It is so scary. It's also amazing. I have settled in here, so I have no need for it.

You know this history professor here I've given it to. He's young, smart, and brave. He also happens to be a hero, in my opinion. Jimmy may just change the world.

We were smoking weed outside a coffee shop. I asked him what he would do with a time machine. He said he would kill Hitler and then save MLK. Good answer. I must say.

So, if you had a magic genie lamp you didn't want to use anymore, would you let it go to waste? I don't think I will either. This has been a critical decision. Please believe it. Just the thought of Jimmy succeeding makes me want to give him this chance to use the Glowbox. This guy could maybe redo history for the better.

I know I made up my mind to give Jimmy the box basically the night I met him. I just lurked around, watching him from the background. I guess I was evaluating him to see if he really was the most accurate candidate. Observing this beautiful specimen was easier said than done because he was knee-deep in the cool kids, and then there's me, an unusual face in the background.

Kill Hitler and save MLK sounds like one heck of a plan. I believed he would do the best with it. Can you just imagine your life today if those two things had happened? What kinds of differences would be incredibly obvious?

Less hate and more love, what a concept, right? That question had been asked to many people by me. You know, what would you do with a time machine? Most folks had such self-centered answers. Most people I asked would go back and save a relationship, or a relative, or even a pet. This guy went right for the meat and potatoes. He shot straight for World Peace, or at least a crack at it. I believe he can't miss.

I couldn't knock his hustle, in fact, I loved where his head was at. So, I studied him to make sure I wasn't making a mistake. The Glowbox is far too powerful to just be destroyed. There's way too much potential in it to change the flow of some trouble spots in history. My military background made it easy to track him. My friendship with a great weed dealer made it even easier. I had far less difficult of a time interviewing him when he was stoned. He had no idea he was being interviewed to be the next man to travel through time.

The guy was army trained and stoner-brained. He's a genius when it comes to Sociology and World History for sure. I had been toying with the notion too long of passing it on before I disappeared into the Sixties, never to be heard from again. I just did it.

I just knew the Glowbox was far too amazing to destroy. In

the right hands, it could change the course of history, which is why it was invented. The box being used by a normal hero instead of for military purposes could be an incredible event.

The thought of simply dismantling it and erasing it from existence was what I first settled on after all the crap I went through with it. There's just too much potential for amazing outcomes for that. I believe in my decision. I stand by Jimmy.

Chapter 2: Home Sweet Home

Sweetie, my first plan was to scatter each part across the Pacific. I decided to stay in this little gorgeous chunk of the bay. Home Sweet Home. What if someone finds it and this futuristic piece of metal ends up on the news?

It wouldn't matter, I guess because I would be away from it and not be able to be linked to it. I don't want the technology to be found and create this dramatic mess because of it going to the wrong hands. I just kept the dang thing hidden forever, Rose. I finally went to drop it in the ocean and stumbled into Chuckie and now you.

That's how we got here to ole Jimmy boy. I've decided to pass this thing down like an old ball hat that's just too sentimental to trash. Will he want this crazy gift, though? I had no choice but to use it.

Jumping time, in my case, was a rash decision, to say the least. He'll have the choice to pass and if he doesn't, we can prepare him for his travels. I knew, in the right hands, the Glowbox could drastically reshape terrible moments in history. Sweetie, the Army man in me wouldn't let its power be squandered!

How to present this thing was a serious conflict. How do you ask someone if they want a time machine? It almost cost me my ass a couple of times, but it didn't. I'm sitting right here talking to you now, Rose, so it all worked out.

Selfish purposes are all I could come up with for the machine. I'm no better than the slew of rejected candidates I secretly interviewed. I didn't want to save a cat or a life with a former romantic partner. I used it to escape into an era I imagined my entire life.

I know there's going to be some preparation necessary for him to use this thing. I'll have to teach him how to charge it and how to use it. I'll have to show him the best way to deal with how it makes you feel physically. The way it affects you mentally I believe is far more trying, however.

I'm done with it for sure. The bay area during this beautiful time period is my final resting place. I'm going to spend all the rest of my days tooling around Haight Street, smoking weed and shopping for tie-dyes. After all, I went through to scurry here, this seems like living in a colorful, energized painting of the past. I'm not ever leaving.

You know how you feel coming home after a long day of work? Amplify that by a million. That's how I feel right now in San Francisco. Before I truly begin to call this place home, I have to settle this issue with the Glowbox. This guy Jimmy is in for the ride of his life if he accepts. I'm about to disappear into the realm of Sixties San Francisco gladly and never return. This must be done. I want to do it with a clear conscience.

Getting stoned with him was how I decided on him as a candidate. I concluded that's the best way to confront him about the Glowbox. Ok, my first hurdle is this: getting him alone. Rose this guy is like the social director at Berkeley.

Jimmy hangs out with the cool crowd seven nights a week. I was worried I may have to spring this thing on him out in public. I met you and you volunteered to take me to him. I don't blame you. I would want to watch someone travel through time too.

I had rapped with him at a bunch of parties and get-togethers. It's not like we met up for lunch or anything. So, I schemed up a good idea to really get him baked. We could spring the idea on him of traveling through time, then.

I had to get up with Chuckie for some weed. That's been my angle on Jimmy. So, that's where I started with my approach about him taking the Glowbox. I needed Chuckie and found you!

You know he's your typical total southern California hippy/surfer. Off to the beach I go. Bolinas up to Stinson beach are usually the spots where I find him. Felt good that day to put my toes in the sand that day and get started.

These beaches are gorgeous! Beautiful clear light blue water wrapping around the most relaxing shade of dark beige sand you can imagine. It's hardly comparable to the Upper Peninsula. I do not miss Michigan or Georgia.

Seeing as how I can't get a license because my social security number won't be issued for like another thirty years, I had to take the bus from downtown. The ride is just as gorgeous; seeing the high rises turn into Chinatown and roll out to the beach is a treat. The trip is surely more interesting than most you can take in northern Michigan, that's for sure.

Having a blast mingling with some of the surfers and just looking for my buddy made me waste most of the day I met you. We were drinking beers and smoking on the beach, but hey, who's complaining? This place is so beautiful. All I had to say was that I was looking for Chuckie and everyone was nice to me.

Once I made my way over to Stinson Beach, I ran into this girl who wanted to talk to Chuckie too. She's a cute, tan, long legged drink of water in cutoff shorts and a flower bikini top and nothing else, thank goodness. You may know her ... Rose, Red Rose. Ha-ha.

You're so awesome. One of the surfers there told you he was up at Crescent Beach, and you said I could ride up there with you, what a sweetie. You looked at me while we were finishing our beers and told me I was cute, but before I could make it out of my shock to respond, you started running towards your van and shouting, "Come on!"

Far be it me to let a woman like you down, so I grabbed up my backpack and my beer and hauled off after you as fast as humanly possible. I was not about to miss a second with this gorgeous little beach creature. You had me wrapped from the start! You truly had me at hello.

You walk like a baby deer with those long, strong, graceful legs. Trust me, if you have blood in your veins and have any desire for females, you'd study the way this gorgeous little Goddess moved too. Watching your long hair blow in the ocean breeze really got to me.

You know now why I was so serious about you taking me to Chuckie. I needed that weed to get to Jimmy. That night was so perfect. You made me settle on giving that damn box away instantly and staying here with you.

It was a no-brainer after that first night we spent looking for him. By midnight I had forgotten about all about that whole mess for the first time since the night this crap happened. Thank you so much for that, Rose. I mean it when I say you take my mind completely from the whole Glowbox fiasco.

That machine has been an all-consuming void in my life since the second I saw it. Thanks to you it's my past and now you're my future. Let me tell you, sweetheart, I couldn't be happier. The beach life in your van would be such an interesting parallel to traveling with the box.

I wouldn't change it for the world, in fact, I could've changed it for anywhere in the world; any time in the world, but I chose to be right here with you. I could go to any time and place on Earth, and I want to be right here in this park with you.

Ok, so if you could give up any time and place to be with me, would you? That's exactly what I did to be with you. Just keep that in mind when I start getting on your nerves, lol. I could be anywhere in the history of mankind and I'm sitting on this bench with you, staring at this van.

Speaking of your van, where should we park it tonight? I wouldn't mind sleeping at the beach in Crescent City. You know, that's where I popped up when I sent myself here. It's where I fell in love with you, too. We could go there after the Dead show.

That's my lucky spot here, for sure. I picked the countryside out there for a few reasons, really. It would be a great place to spend the night, let's go there. I picked that spot because of the desolation. Coming out of the woods onto that beautiful beach was incredible.

I'll tell you all about these crazy journeys tonight out there by the fire. We should get going soon after the show. I want to make it out there in time to gather some firewood. I suggest we knock out these burritos and hit the road. I can't wait to get back out to the beach with you and just relax under the stars.

You'll have to drive us out there, remember? Do you have to treat me like a fugitive on the run? My social security number won't be created for a very long time. I must use this fake identification to prove myself to the authorities. It does work, though.

I know I sound crazy as a loon with all this. You know better now. That's why I'm taking you out there. I left proof of my journey to this time out there in case I ever needed to prove this to anyone. That's where I'd like to put it back.

I'm glad you know I'm not crazy and just have an insane story about how I ended up here. Red, you are a keeper of epic proportions. Since you've seen this, the way I live will make sense to you. I was so nervous going out there with you.

I'm not crazy and I'm not on the run. I'm an accidental gypsy of the ancient tribe of yours from the future. You're the reason I'm leaving the caravan. So, sweetie, I know this is all blows your mind, but now you know the truth. You know, deep down in your heart I'm not full of it.

Let's talk about us on the way there. Do you think you can get used to seeing my ugly mug every morning when you wake up? I can wake up in this van looking at the tide roll in every morning with you for sure, which is why I'm taking you here to bury this again. I'm putting so much trust in you. I want to wake up in sandy blankets with burrito wrappers with you in here forever.

Honestly, I'm terrified for you to know about this. I know this rocks your world far more than any trip you've been on with acid. This is my proof to you that I'm not some psycho on the run from a scary past, though.

It's such a pretty drive up the coast. When I first got here, I camped on the beaches quietly, just trying to make my way down into the city. It sucked sometimes because I had to beg to eat. My money was no good here.

I thought about passing some of it off to unsuspecting street venders, in hopes to make change for money I could spend. I was just too worried about it being linked back and me getting tracked down. I just drifted on down the coast like the other bums.

I'm really used to taking care of myself, so the panhandling was seriously a humbling experience. I've never really had to depend on the kindness of others, except for my parents when I was growing up. Looking back, there were a few times I should've helped people in need in my past and it shows. I was really hoping to eat a couple nights out there on the beach and no one would feed me. While I was laying there holding my belly, I swear I saw a slide show of every homeless person I walked right past in my life!

Chapter 3: Better Pay Grade

When I made it to the city, it was easier to get food. The streets were full of vagabond hippies, so I just blended in with them. I slept where they slept and ate what they ate. They taught me plenty; believe me.

I have the same rights as an illegal alien now, which are none. More than that, I cannot prove who I am at all, which is scary. I was completely terrified the few times I got jumped onto by cops. This fake identity has proven to be a life saver.

I found a good way to take care of myself as a laborer for a guy who does construction. I've been renting a little room from an older couple who just want to see a little cash every month and no identification. I've finally gotten myself a little groove going here where I've gotten as comfortable as possible. This is one of the main reasons I decided to ditch the Glowbox. Really, it's how I stumbled up on you too.

Now, here we are driving this sweet little van up the coast, you make me feel complete. I love it with you. You're so pretty, Red. I'm a lucky guy to be by your side. I've had a blast with you this short time we've been together.

I really hope I'm making the right decision by showing you what I've shown you. I was a nervous wreck bringing you out here to show you the phone and explain the Glowbox. I'll never forget it. I still remember rehearsing my story.

I first jumped time on May 26, 2009. It was a complete accident. I had no intention of leaving my life in the past, of course. That's just the way the cookie crumbled. I am here with you by an incredible twist of fate.

I was an MP. You know what that means, right... military police. I was just trying to spend my time in the army, collect my pension, and settle down one day somewhere. Ending up in Golden Gate Park with a beautiful hippy girl in 1968 was not quite on my radar. How could it have been? Nevertheless, he we are. I couldn't be happier about it either.

I woke up and made some coffee, just like any other day. The day I found the Glowbox, though, was not anything close to ordinary. My life would never be the same. My plans to go to the lake for Memorial Day weekend changed drastically, to say the least.

I was really doing well in my role as an MP. I was in my tenth year of military police work. I had made my way up to staff sergeant. I wasn't the boss of my base, I was, however, the leader of my unit. That's way better than not being a boss.

Five years of being night commander at Fort Benning was very boring most of the time. We handled a bunch of rowdy young guys, mostly. I was pretty good at it, though. Believe it or not, they weren't that bad, usually. We dealt with mostly fist fights over drinking or girls, possibly both, and occasional theft.

It only took me three years to become night commander by default. I lucked into it, but really took it seriously, so I had a great reputation. Those night shifts at Fort Benning are how I ended up with the Glowbox. The Glowbox is how I ended up here.

The Air Force had some sort of security team training with the Green Berets for years. They only trained at night, but other than that, I really didn't think anything strange about their routine. I assumed it was mostly about Jedi training on a different level than me, so I smiled and nodded and let them do their thing.

I ended up with a time machine because I minded my own business. Apparently, I was so good at it Night Fox company noticed. The name of their team just sounded sneaky, I always thought. Their patch is a fox riding a lightning bolt out of the moon. It's neat.

These guys were really on another level. They were up to some ninja space science, for sure. I'm sitting on a park bench with a beautiful young woman in the year 1968. That patch really makes perfect sense now. I'll always wonder if they will be able to track me down because of the Glowbox. I'm curious if they have a way to locate it.

The base I jumped time from was Warner Robbins Air Force Base. Bossing those night shifts at Fort Benning was getting so old. I was complaining about it one night to the commander of the Night Foxes. He heard me.

The poor guy was just trying to get out of the gate, and I was going on and on about feeling like a high school principal watching a bunch of kids. He offered me a job guarding their section at Robbins immediately. I really wanted a more serious assignment, and he said I was perfect for a spot with them. Starting again at the bottom of the totem pole was the only thing I was dreading.

Sweetie, this was such a better paygrade it was impossible to turn down. It took me two months to get free from my sergeant responsibilities and move to security for Night Foxes. That's fast for military time, especially for a move like that. I was in good with my commanders. I had to wait for my replacement to be trained and for my position to be arranged in their section.

The only spot they had open was just at the bottom level. The plan was to work my way up to chief of their security. It did not work out that way. I found the Glowbox and now here we are.

My first gig, of course, was lame. It was the third shift guard of their smallest building, but it had the best security systems on the doors. This always raised my curiosity. Then I started thinking big things come in small packages.

They were up my ass too. You don't sit down for twelve hours a day. You are basically on a continued loop patrol for twelve straight hours. It was hardcore. Whatever was behind those doors was valuable, I knew that.

I was finally free of wrestling young privates and recruits and sorting out a bunch of booze-fueled nonsense, which was awesome. Plus, I had the potential to really move up in here rank which is always a better pay scale. No one usually dislikes more pay.

Thank goodness Warner Robbins had been a base for a while. When I jumped time, I popped back up at the same location on base and was able to charge the Glowbox. My coordinates were set back to the same place. That spot was in the middle of a field back then.

You must recharge it every time you use it. Jumping into a time before electricity would mean you're stuck. Unless you bring some type of charging station that can do it for you. I did not.

I had to sneak around Robbins for a couple of days to get it charged. I had to hide and starve for a while to get it charged. Really good thing security cameras were in prehistoric days then. I would've been out of luck if they weren't.

I'm glad I was a stoner, or I would've had no idea where to hide and plug it in. I used to sneak into this old hangar to smoke weed when I got used to my routine. That's how I remember this old air conditioner. Turns out it was brand new in 1959. The building, I mean.

That hangar turned out to be my lifeline. I stole food from the employee's lunches in the fridge. I found an old, greasy mechanic's coveralls and wore those. It took a couple of days to charge the device. I had time to think and decided my time and place was where I wanted to be.

I would've surely been exposed if I had to appear in front of people. I only had to interact with people of that time twice. I passed a guy right after I put the coveralls on. He barely noticed me or the bag I was carrying which contained my modern clothes.

The only thing that was even said to me was, "Welcome to Hell." I guess the guy thought I was a new mechanic and said that to me in passing. I just nodded and said "thanks". I was so nervous when he popped around the corner. I'm still surprised it wasn't painfully obvious.

It was hard as hell to sneak in there. Turns out Warner Robbins was a good secure base then too. I was in shock when I first jumped! Thank God I ended up in a field at first. I was really shaken up. Took me some time to even begin to get my bearings. I was very dizzy, having vertigo and nausea symptoms. I'm sure you can imagine that.

I thought I had set the machine back fifty minutes, but no, I jumped back fifty years! I ended up in 1959. You can imagine my surprise. I had like twenty minutes to look at the instructions before I had to use it. So, I hope that explains my error.

I was kind of in a rush since I had to escape these Night Fox commandos. These guys are intimidating as Hell, you must understand. They were the elite of two branches of service. These guys are real USDA-certified badasses!

I was just an MP, and these guys were hardcore elite

assassins. I had to run. They would have really messed me up. Imagine if they had caught me with that thing.

They still might. I don't know if they have some way to track the box. I guess we'll find out soon enough. That's been my biggest fear. I'm terrified these guys will find me and throw me in a shallow grave where I'll never be heard from again.

I know I'll never be heard from again in 2009. Who knows what tale had been told of my demise back there already? There was certainly a cover-up. No one was told I found a time machine and used it, I'm certain.

Chapter 4: Welcome to the Fifties

I wonder what sad story they passed on to my family after I disappeared with the Glowbox. I must admit I'm curious how they got away with a closed casket, or did they say I've simply disappeared? Did I have a funeral? Did they simply claim I was missing?

My poor mama probably worries herself sick about me or believes I'm dead. There's nothing I can do right now. She is alive currently. I know; however, I cannot interact with her. God only knows what type of disruption it would cause.

There's no way to make sure she wouldn't look at the info I provided as soon as I walked away. So many ideas flowed through my head about what to tell her. Warnings of the inevitable tragedies to come could only throw off her timeline in unimaginable ways. I couldn't give her info for the future.

A letter that would be given to me when I joined the military is what I thought about giving her. There's no way the letter would reach its intended destination. That letter would inevitably be opened prematurely.

Meeting her in my adult body would have to cause some kind of effect. A lady meeting her adult son decades before he's even conceived would be off the charts. Face to face contact is out. How could I have passed on the info anonymously?

I don't think that's an irrational fear. A bunch of special forces soldiers making you disappear seems very scary to me now. Does it to you? I already disappeared. They could deal me a fate worse than death and there's nothing that could do about it.

I'll have to let her believe the story the military told her. Thoughts of ways to warn her seem futile and extremely dangerous. There's no way to be sure she won't see my message before the appointed time. I guess the military dealt the tale of my fate to her and there's nothing I can do.

I lay in that field for a while, trying to plot my next move. I was so scared they would jump with a Glowbox right behind me and wipe me out right in that field, but they didn't. I kept seeing visions of them coming out of nowhere and shooting me in the head.

That whole night I just tried to shake visions of dying from a .9mm slug, lying face down in that rainy Georgia field. Did I have only one? Could they have more? Could they track mine?

Thank goodness the technology was so experimental I literally had to have the only one, or I would've been a dead man for sure Rose. I had ghastly fantasies about what they would do to me. I was terrified about getting tortured while being questioned about what I had done while I had the machine.

The first night I was back in the 50s, I just looked at the stars I could see around the rainclouds, trying not to think about what would happen to me if the Night Foxes found me. I was more afraid of what they would do to me than the fact that I had time-traveled to a completely different time. That's crazy, huh? I am still terrified.

I only believed it was a time machine after I used it. Obviously, I had missed some important instructions because I jumped back fifty years instead of fifty minutes! I was laying in that field most of the night, wondering what time period I was even in. Thank goodness 110 power was existent in the 50's.

I just laid by this tree, hoping someone wasn't going to come to check out the light and noise that had to happen when I jumped time. What kind of physical changes happened in their time when I was entering it? Who knows?

I was just lying there pondering in the stars intensely. This ole boy was terribly curious about what year it was. It then hit me... what year do I want it to be? I eventually chose 1968 and here we are, trying to figure out what to do now, after we've just given away a time machine.

You are an amazing girl, Rosie. I hope you don't ditch me now. Lord knows you can have any man you want. I'll be a lucky one if it's me you want. That's a fact.

I know now that you've seen what you've seen, and at least you can't think I am full of shit. I can't lie to you and tell you

I'm not paranoid about what I've shown you. You may decide telling everyone is your best bet. You could turn me into the cops.

I didn't plan on meeting you. I only tried to come to your day and age. I have done that. I hope that we can do something together. I just know that I was happier in that hammock with you than any other time in my life. I'm simply trying to be happy with you and run with that.

Sitting there in that field I really mulled some thoughts over. That's how I started concluding that this era is where I want to be. Imagine being able to pick a time and place to go. I was given that gift.

I had to give up everything I had known. It was honestly a no-brainer. Getting rid of this machine once I got settled was on the top of my list. The Sixties were the place for me.

Life happens so fast. I got a crazy chance to start mine over in the era of my choosing. I picked this place and ran into you. I fell hard for you and now the ball is totally in your court. I want to spend this time here with you. What are you going to do?

It's not much further, it's on this side of Crescent City. I wouldn't mind having a few beers for this, trust me, you wouldn't either. Would you stop at the next gas station and let me grab some? We'll be getting off the main road soon and heading into the woods.

I absolutely love going into the gas stations of this time. It's a real reminder of the technology gap. Most of the ads are glossy paper not crazy printed 3D vinyl stickers. The coolers are all on the ground not doors built into the walls.

There's no cooler after cooler energy drinks (which are caffeine and sugar-filled drinks made to speed you up) and specialized coffees and sodas. I hope I have a picture of a gas station from my day on this phone somewhere.

I enjoy the plain logos and simple color schemes and the old registers. It makes me think of the blinking and dinging computerized versions I was used to. I know California is always kind of ahead of the curve, so I could only imagine what's being used in the high country of Montana right now.

So many of the products on the shelves have such vague labeling. Also, a big thing that stands out to me is that most of the packaging isn't cellophane or plastic. There's still so much cardboard and paper. The bottles here are still glass. It's just miles and miles of plastic in my time.

What kind of beer do you drink? If Budweiser is fine, I'll just grab that. You must promise me that you'll keep quiet about what you've seen even if you decide it freaks you out. I don't care if you decide to drive away screaming, please don't say anything.

I'm really going out on a limb here, so I must trust you big time. You're the first person I've felt like I could trust since all this started. That's the only reason you are seeing all this!

I want a partner. I want what folks call a soul mate. Spending the rest of my life with my best friend sounds amazing. You seem like you would make an amazing lover and best friend.

While I was gathering firewood, I pondered how to spring this on you. I was thinking about having some beers and a few smokes first. I was working up all these different angles to present this to you.

There wasn't really any pitch that would work well. I just showed it to you. Oops... that sounded kind of dirty. I figure it'll take a few beers to even try to deal with all this. We might as well get started. Imagine a computer, only the size of a notebook or even smaller than just a phone receiver... I'm about to blow your mind.

When I first got here, I knew I had to stash this thing. My name is Allen Ferguson, but you'll have to call me Robert Miller to everyone else. I`ve shown you my portable phone from the future, called a cell phone.

Now, here we are out in these beautiful woods. I'm showing you why I'm living under an assumed name. This was my phone I used in the 2000s before I jumped through time. I hid it here after the Glowbox brought me here.

What you've seen is like nothing you'll ever see again for twenty more years. I'm sure it seems alien to you. I've spent so much time back here now it almost seems alien to me.

Chapter 5: Pure Simple Love

My cell phone is wild, huh? It's like the phone at your parents' house, but it works everywhere and acts as a computer. Computers are still so uncommon these days that you have absolutely no idea of their full capabilities. It's powering on, so when this boots up, your mind's about to continue to be blown. Here's a beer, drink up it's about to be an interesting night.

The first time my home screen came on, I watched your eyes light up like Christmas Day on the mother ship. This is called the home screen and it's where you open all your apps. Every one of these little symbols has a different function on the phone. Apps are short for applications. Applications are the functions your phone and or computer can do.

There's really nothing in this era for me to compare to, so I just let you play with it. This one is my gallery, it's where my pictures are. Oh, it acts as a camera too. It keeps all the pictures stored inside it, instead of them all having to be printed on paper. I can connect my phone to a bigger computer a couple of different ways and print my pictures or whatever is needed if I want.

Looking through all these pictures I wanted you to really pay attention to all the details. I'll explain whatever you want to know about these. You pick them with your fingers like this... it's called a touch screen. You use your finger like a mouse on a regular computer. I know this is so foreign to you, but in the era I grew up in, this is commonplace.

Like I told you, it's called a cell phone, that's short for a cellular phone. Most people have them in my days. There is also a wide variation of similar devices that can run these applications. Also, all types of machines can be controlled by these devices. A lot will change in the way of technology over the next fifty or sixty years. We have plenty of time for us to play with this phone.

I showed you this because I really want to stay together with you, and I needed you to know I'm not insane or just a fugitive. I'll answer any questions you have about the Glowbox or my phone. I was hoping to enjoy this gorgeous night with you and hopefully get to just hold you again now that you see the truth about me. I've still got my fingers crossed, praying you don't high tail it out of the woods completely freaked out.

You just checked that phone out while we relaxed in this hammock. It's cool watching you see this for the first time. You've now seen something absolutely no one alive has ever possibly seen, that must be very cool. That's why I'm kind of putting pressure on you to know how much I like you, because this is serious. I just made you the first person to ever see a cellphone. That's freaking cool.

Oh, you want to know who that is with her arms around me? That's my ex-girlfriend. She must be an ex now because I'm fifty years away from her. I'm glad you think she's pretty. I think you're way prettier, though, and way cooler.

The look in your eye says my little line worked.... yay. Still, amazed by my hopes of snuggling with you turned into the hottest night of my life! So, I guess you believe me and are thinking about being serious with me, too. "I hope you don't do the things you did with me last night with just any body you're hanging out with. That little love tap of a slap on the cheek says it all... ok. Good, you're really into me. I'm happy about that.

I'm incredibly glad I found Chuckie that day for all kinds of reasons. I needed the weed to butter this Jimmy kid up for the proposition of a lifetime. Since he took the machine, we can run away together, and I can really settle in here and not have this burden on my shoulders. I can't wait.

I can honestly say I want nothing more than to be rid of this thing, but I couldn't just destroy it. The Glowbox is too powerful! Guess we'll have to get back to the beach soon and find this wild man, Chuckie. We're going to need more weed before we go watch the Dead.

I'm so glad I couldn't find him earlier and we ended up together. You are the best company I've ever had in my life, Rose. If you can hang with me for a little while longer, I'm going to blow your mind again in more ways than one. I'll be the best man you'll ever have.

You know Chuckie better than me, where could we look? You said you know where he lives. Do you think we could go there? Is that ok?

Regardless, I can settle down right here in sunny California. Reflecting on tonight makes me hope it's with you, that's for sure. I'll be the luckiest man I know if you don't leave me. Is that how you feel?

You`ve just played with the phone, imagine if we used the Glowbox. I have an actual time machine! Well, at least I will when he gets back. Do you think he'll come back?

We should get some breakfast on the way back out here. I could sure use a breakfast burrito. I think it's going to be a long day. I have some amazing acid. Will you take some with me?

We'll need some fuel in our bellies for sure. Let's bury this phone out here and go to the Dead show. I'll drive back to town. No problem.

The way things went down in that hammock makes me glad to see this machine change hands. You are an amazing woman. I'm not sure if I care if he even brings the thing back. Nothing would please me more than being free of my phone and the Glowbox.

Jimmy is entertaining this idea of how to use this machine to make good things happen. The whole time we were apart I was training him. You saw a man travel back in time, that's how much I trust you.

More nights like this one are what is required for my

happiness. Without the futuristic equipment lying around I can finally relax and just feel at home. I would sure love to feel at home with a sweetie like you. I'm almost there.

Feeling a little less like a fugitive on the run will be amazing. Falling asleep and holding you under the stars in the hammock was the happiest time of my life, sweetie. The fire was dwindling down, and you were snoozing, and I felt like a king. You smell like flowers and honey and sunshine. I love it.

I fell completely in love with you while you were sleeping. I was scared I was going to squeeze you so tight you would wake up! I lived our whole life in my head before falling asleep. It was beautiful.

A life of actual obtainable bliss is what was generated too. You still looked incredible fifty years from now. You looked so pretty in your little dresses working in your garden. A life filled with pure, simple love is a life worth living.

It didn't take long to see how beautiful your heart and soul are. The look in your eye radiates warmth and damn, it's beautiful. Your past can simply become your past in an instant. The future can show up to take you on for the ride of your life, if you're receptive and ready to move forward.

You're going to need to buckle up, though, it may go fast and hard at times. Progress is not always easy. You cannot move effectively forward if you're stuck looking behind. That's a fact. Your past is your past for a reason; leave it there.

When life makes you uncomfortable, it may be for a reason. You wouldn't move if you didn't have to sometimes! I'm trying to just roll with all these changes and just find real happiness. Busting, burning, and burying this phone right here wouldn't bother me one bit.

My past will always be the future, but it's like it didn't happen now. It didn't happen, or at least, it didn't happen yet. I pray to whoever is listening that future is here in the past with you by my side. I've never prayed harder for anything.

Chapter 6: James Bond Eat Your Heart Out

I still find it hard to believe that while I was busy falling in love with you, you were trying to figure out how to ditch me and steal my phone. I was certain you were some MKULTRA worker. I was terrified you had let me get dosed and turned me into the F.B.I. They use pretty girls like you to trick people into LSD experiments right now in this town.

MKULTRA is a top-secret government program going on now where hippy girls trick people into being test subjects. They trick them into taking LSD and doing mind-control experiments. It's going on all over your town right now, you just don't know about it. Or do you? They called it Operation Midnight Climax.

The government is all over San Francisco right now using sexy girls like you to lore unsuspecting people into places under false pretenses. It's terrifying because they are dosing them with pure LSD without their knowledge and letting people conduct experiments on them. You see the beauty of this experience when you take it with your friends. Imagine them using it for terrible things right under our noses, and they are.

The time I come from knows this as a fact. The C.I.A. was part of this too. Eventually, they used this research to make trained assassins and operatives. They called them Manchurian Candidates. They use them to do all types of dirty work.

They called them Manchurian Candidates because of the island of Manchuria, which is where the US literally bought an island full of Feudal outlaw farmers. They blocked the island off, mostly, and slowly farmers started disappearing. Terrible experiments were done on these poor people. The mind control program known as MKULTRA was one of the main results.

Modern Manchurian Candidates were people who could put suggestions and thoughts into the minds of and make them do anything basically. They did it using weird signals. They taught the people to even commit murder and then return into some other blank head space and in some cases, have amnesia for what they'd done! It is very scary.

I don't blame you, though. Thank goodness you just showed it to your mom. She's cool. She'll keep her mouth shut about it, I'm sure. I get it; you have this alien technology in your hands, and you want to run with it. It's totally understandable.

I was born in 1983, and I grew up in an era where bull crap just doesn't cut it. We have the internet in my day, and we'll find out the truth because you can just look it up. There's not a lot of ways to hide information in my day. You just type someone's name in a box and find them. You can find out anything you want about a person.

The one place you messed up was telling me how good of friends you are with Chuckie. Thank God for that or I may never have found you. I 'm trying to spend the rest of my life with a woman like you. I couldn't have expected you to know that then, but sweetie, you do now.

My real name is Allen Ferguson, but I guess you can get used to calling me Robert Miller. I'm not going to lie. While I was looking for you, I was really kicking myself for showing you the phone. Terrified can't even come close to explaining how I felt. I tried not to even imagine where you had taken it.

Having the balls to take off with the phone makes me love you that much more, however. That gives me the impression you're maybe tough enough to hang with me through all of this. You can help me keep my cover if the shit really hits the fan. It just may.

I really need a rebel spirit in my companion. The rest of my life here will have to be lived incognito. Extreme measures have been taken on my part to blend in as best as possible, but all my time here will be spent on the lamb. I'm ready for it, though.

Handing over the keys to the realm of time and space should be enough to give us peace of mind. I'm no longer responsible for this power no one should ever have... or should they? I believe he is going to change the course of mankind for the better. We can ride off into the sunset in your little van.

You heard him; he's got some amazing ideas of which to use the box. I really have faith in him. Can you imagine if he does kill Hitler or save MLK or JFK? Any of those would be a total rewrite of the evolution of human consciousness. You know that's the truth.

I thought so hard about trying to take on a monumental mission like that when I chose to come here. I instead just opted for a sweet, peaceful, beautiful existence. Rose, now here we are. I'm all yours. Treat me well.

He'll probably never come back here. Will our whole world just suddenly change if Jimmy does it? Will we just go to sleep and wake up with the whole black rights movement warped in a huge stretch our minds can't even fathom? MLK was really on a roll, that's why they killed him.

Could we take a bath and come out of the bathroom and the lifelines of billions of people who weren't executed catch up? There's a whole lot of brilliant European people out there. What types of changes will have taken place? We only have knowledge of how things have been up till now in this established reality.

This is really getting into some serious mind-blowing science-fiction thought patterns and I love it. How will what we know to be fact now intertwine with the changes that come from his actions? Millions upon millions of lives could be changed for the better. The world could change in a literal heartbeat.

It's impossible for me to even wrap my head around this. I don't believe I should. He took the box and used it, though; the door was open for sure. Success in his missions means huge differences.

I'm not smart enough to blend into a completely far-off time and culture. Jimmy is, he'll pull this off. I feel it. Tell me that was not the coolest thing you ever watched; for him to just disappear like that, right you can't. It was awesome to just watch it and not experience it.

The way that blue light enveloped him was amazing. That was a real disappearance act. Every magician in the world would be jealous of that. It feels so good for that damn machine to be gone.

I may have just created a rift in time that could make the world a far better place. It may make it completely implode on itself. We really can't be sure. That's intense.

You know how hard it is to sit back and relax and know you created a huge shift in time. That's exactly what I'm going to do, though. I will have to try to shake off all this craziness I was raised in and relax and be a part of the sixties. I'm going to count my blessings for it too.

I grew up in a way more hectic time. I'm about to try and be a part of this era. I only fantasized about it for most of my adult life. Sixties life, you know hippy life was one I dreamed about. Here I am.

Jimmy has a pretty iron-clad plan. MLK hasn't been dead for that long. So, he's going to go to Atlanta in 1967, just a year shy of his death. That's a good plan to show him around his house.

He's going to tell him at his home. There will be a better chance to speak to him alone. Taking the articles from the New York Times and the LA Times should prove it. You saw the memorial coin he found to show him too.

He told you about the news articles he downloaded to his tablet to show him, also. Just the tablet should be enough proof to Dr. King that Jimmy really came from the future. Wouldn't you think? It was for you.

He took a copy of each of those for JFK, as well as a coin. He's going to catch JFK back in Massachusetts before he's elected president. It would be too hard to interact with him after he's elected. He is going to tell him to warn his brother about his assassination too.

What a shame he must go to one of New England's most beautiful locations in its heyday. He'll have to try and hob knob with a Kennedy. Sounds like a fun mission to me, James Bond eat your heart out. Those boys knew how to have a good time!

Chapter 7: The Hammock

Our lives changed forever that night in the hammock. You and I both know it. I fell in love. You were distracted by your psychedelic alien experience, at first.

I'm glad you came around and joined me after being caught. I can never blame you for ditching me. I'm not mad. I probably would've done the same thing.

Looking back, I surely would've done the same thing. Eighteen-year-old me would've taken a space phone and ran too. Our love was born before your instinct to run with it kicked in. This ole boy is thankful for that.

True love doesn't find you for the first time every day. Some folks never seem to find much of it. Most of them take complete advantage of its presence. However, I'm not going to.

Those stars were slowly making their nightly laps over our finely tuned frequency-saturated heads and our luck changed. The rest of the universe went on about its business. We got lucky, in every sense of the word.

I will grow old with you here Rose. I have no longing to

return to the time I left. My mom has already grieved and started a life without me. I had no children or real attachments. We are completely free to move through this time together.

The point I'm really trying to make is that you'll never have to worry about me becoming regretful or homesick. Choosing to come here was an excellent decision. You literally landing in my lap on that hammock was one of the best things to ever happen to me.

You fell asleep in my arms for a while before you woke up and ditched me to steal the phone. I was studying every freckle on your beautiful little face in the moonlight when you did. You had me wrapped around your little finger before you even woke back up.

I did not expect to wake up to a manhunt, or sexy little surfer girl hunt. I had all these visions of us waking up together in the early morning sun, making love again, and destroying the phone before we left the woods. I played with your sweet-smelling strawberry hair and kissed your forehead.

The state of mind I was in had me flashing to visions of old us on a porch swing, with the surf splashing in the background. I am so happy this is still a possibility for us. Waking up to the scenario you left me in threw me for quite a loop. Especially, after a night of something I can only describe as ethereal bliss, I was in a state beyond shock.

There were moments it seemed like we were one entity entangled in physical connection. Nothing short of pure beauty is how I try to compartmentalize the experience. That's the way it will always remain.

Your beautiful little body catching shimmers of the moonlight is so intertwined in my memories. There's no way I would change it for the world. You gave me one of my favorite memories that night.

Your cute girly squeals and moans just add to the soundtrack along with forest encapsulating us. I hear them plain as day when I think back on the hammock. Hearing you describe our connection with the cosmos, in a blurt, while regaining your breath is still so fresh. Like it was moments ago, not weeks.

I'm not too sure I had felt true emotional attachment before that. My whole perception of relationships changed instantaneously. My idea of true connection became irreplaceably altered in an instant. The next morning was more about finding my first source of true love than finding my phone.

You are the most beautiful thing I've ever seen. Physically, of course you're shaped like a goddess, but I mean the way you see the world. I mean the way you made me see the world, as well as the universe. The entire way you view life is so different than the attitudes I'm accustomed to from my time.

Drifting off to sleep that night I felt like the king of the jungle. I felt like the head lion who had finally found his favorite lioness. Waking up alone I instantly felt so paranoid and terrified. Somehow that still was not more powerful than the residual love I was left with. You did a number on me.

There was no choice but to track you down to get the phone back, but deep down I hoped I wasn't alone with the feeling of a real union. The entire time I was making my way back to you my thoughts were consumed with hopes of what we have right now. Chuckie was going on about whatever, while my mind was on the faint hope we could proceed together. Now here we are.

We just swayed in the breeze while the Milky Way danced in front of our opened eyes. This is how we can spend the rest of our days. We can go from here on out creating memory after memory which is just as magical. We now have this power.

We could create our own little family. I can surely teach them gratitude for the peace and solidarity of undistracted thought. You can teach them how to love each molecule of air and leaf and star, just the way you showed me. These are still days when it's ok not to want to be a part of the herd.

There are so many displaced emotions I'm slowly forgetting. Every day here is like a step in the direction of clarity. You'll never know the overwhelming distant environment I left behind. I'm happy about that. There was no distraction.

We were just our own little whisps in the flow of the universe. I know deep down you were undoubtedly consumed with thoughts of the alien device I had just shown you. Regardless, we were alone in our own sparks of life in an infinite glow. You've never known the buzzing of the hive I grew up in.

I've never been kissed the way you kissed me. I've never felt connected to another human being like that. There were times when I couldn't tell we were in our bodies. LSD is such a powerful force.

The times I came back to the realization that I was a man in a body making love to you were unsettling at times. I would catch my breath and focus through the haze and see you were in the same realm. Rose, it was one of the most beautiful moments of my life. I was more concerned about trying to get you than the paranoia of the phone thing, I want a life that feels like us in the hammock.

I want a lifetime of that moment. You felt it too or you would've just kicked me out and not came along with me on this mission. Once this phone is destroyed there's nothing for me to worry about. I know you will choose my peace of mind over playing with this phone.

The second I saw you after Chuckie and I made our way back to your house looked at me like a deer in the headlights. Every time I see you, I feel whole. The way we felt in the hammock does not have to die. We can keep it alive.

When your hands are on my skin the world lets me know, this is the connection it's intended for me the whole time. I can never describe in words the way it feels when you touch me. Natural is the only possible description. Like I told you, I feel like the king of the jungle and it's awesome.

Let's run with this as far as we can. We may wake up tomorrow to drastically changed reality. Jimmy may set an actual eutopia into existence. We may be the catalysts to a brand-new world. It all started with an amazing night under the stars in the woods, as I suppose many amazing lives together begin.

The way the hallucinations become a part of your memories is so interesting to me. It's like a vivid dream. You recall it like it happened. I guess they are real.

They are real I suppose. When you look back and the scene is saturated with frequencies and color splashes, it makes it real. The fact that we were on a drug, of course, is a factor. However, that's the way your brain will forever recall it.

This is where the lines of "so-called" reality get blurred, and I think it's incredible. I truly do. We remember a night full of quantum entanglement and spiritual oneness. We are left with an experience full of astral sensuality.

That, in no way, makes it less real. The whole world had their recollection of night. It just happens that ours is far more colorful and fuller of space age energy and spiritual electricity. I prefer ours.

That's always been the most interesting thing to me about tripping. Most of the population of the Earth goes on about their experience in a normal frequency. You create a space in yours full of time warps and amazing mystical occurrences. They are both valid and real.

Our experiences are technically labeled as hallucinations or figments of our imagination. We both are experiencing the same movements and charges of color and realm traveling.

Therefore, we must have altered our lives in a way the normal folk won't ever know. Does the fact a chemical made our night completely cosmic and downright spiritual make it any less real?

Turn on, tune in, and drop out. Under the stars, swaying in a hammock, that's exactly what we did. I wouldn't change it for the entire world either. That night, no matter how electrically charged, and color washed it may be, was one of my favorite experiences.

There were times it felt like we were one entwined lifeform just floating in the stars. That is way cooler than just experiencing a normal night under the stars. Occasionally you get lucky. Life is so full of downs it's good to cling to the ups.

That night was surely an up in my book. You are such an amazing human being. Getting to spend my time with you is an absolute blessing. Some folks spend their entire life with a person who brings the whole experience down to a low with them. Our case is the exact opposite.

We have taken things beyond the next level. When you picked me up on the beach you had no idea you were to step into a parallel dimension. Neither did I. I had no intention of showing you a glimpse of the future and falling in love with you.

We were both just trying to find some weed. The universe had a different agenda for us apparently. We never found Chuckie that night. We found love and then thankfully I stumbled upon him the next morning.

He led me right back to you. We were meant to be together. That hammock brought us into a quantum entanglement that is based on love. It feels like I am right where I am supposed to be every second I'm beside you.

The look in your eyes reassures this assumption for me. The spark I feel when you touch my skin lets me know I'm right on track. Jimmy is gone and here I am being shown the bay area by an incredible girl. I feel pretty good about my choices at this point.

I'm going to keep my mouth shut about the future as much as possible. I want the rest of my life to feel like the night in the hammock. I don't want to spend it spilling the ugly truth about a time that Jimmy may drastically change. My time here will be spent absorbing the vibrations of your generation.

The less you know about the future the better. There's plenty of good things to come, but there's just as much you're better off not worrying about. Let's just keep the energy alive we created that night in the hammock. I never intended to tell anyone a thing about the Glowbox or my whole experience.

Here we are now. You know all about the entire thing. I'll tell you as much as you want to know, I really will. Always keep in mind I am far more interested in becoming a part of your world than going on about the one I left behind.

I left a world stuffed completely full of over stimulation for one of easy-going salt water-soaked peace and love. The days I lived in were so full of constant distraction. I would rather you show me the vibration your crowd works on than tell you about mine.

My only regret of that night in the hammock was showing you the phone that night. I wish I had waited till morning. I was consumed with knowing the truth about me for some reason. I'm glad you know.

Chuckie was my savior that morning after you left. He looked like an angel walking across that parking lot, carrying his surfboard, to me. I'm glad he knew where you lived. He kept going on about what a good couple we would make.

I believe he's right. You've been the only thing on my mind since about an hour after I got in the van with you. Our little romp in the hammock out there was the most sensual pleasant moment of my life. You're the best sweetie.

My whole ride back to you I kept returning to thoughts of how beautiful and charming you are. The phone was an issue I had to get resolved immediately. I was still just completely consumed by thoughts of having you in my life, as well.

We made some magic out there in the woods. I'll never be able to see you the same again. To me you'll always be a little tan radiant Goddess. There's no two ways around it.

You're my little Goddess now, I'm a lucky guy. I can be myself around you. I don't have to stay on guard and not let anything slip. That is worth more than anything I can imagine, it's priceless.

I've been living one lie after another since the moment I got here. When we're alone I can let loose. I can talk about this crazy stuff, and you know all about it. You're a part of it.

Since you met me, you have seen a phone from the future and watched a man time travel, all in a week's time. Who else is going to bring adventure like that into your life? It wasn't intentional to bring you completely into this mess. Happens to be that it is also now my saving grace.

Rose you're now my safe haven. When I'm with you I'm in my one place, I don't have to hide the secret past my life. I'm in my one place I don't have to replace the truth about who I am with a barrage of lies. It's so exhausting.

I am a genuinely honest person. You are too. That's the reason you saw the phone the first night we were together. I felt somewhere deep down it was okay to open to you, thank goodness I listened.

I always listen to my gut, always. The army really made us learn to lean on our intuition. Mine told me to spill my guts out under the stars that night. Looking back now, I wouldn't change it for the world.

I do regret not waiting till morning to show you the phone. It's too late now though. We can only move forward from here. I can't wait. A future with you would surely be nothing short of spectacular.

Excitement about the days to come far outweighs any forms of doubt. You've seen the craziest turn of events and you're still here. I you're assume you're here to stay. I hope you're here to stay.

Fantasies of the rest of my days in your arms swirled through my mind that night. That night was the most priceless memory I have. You, Rose, are the most priceless soul I've ever encountered. I hope for a life here with you more than anything I've ever wanted. That's a fact.

You made me feel at home here for the first time. My time here has been spent feeling much more like a convict on the run. You made my attitude about my life here completely flip flop. There will never be a way I can properly thank you.

I forgot all about the whole wild experience that led me to the hammock with you. The hours we spent together were the first ones I felt free in since I came here. Words will never properly describe what you gave me, before you took my phone. My being here came to life the night I met you!

We were just two souls drifting through the cosmos. I wasn't a soldier on the run through time. I wasn't a man living under an assumed identity. I was a soul connected with another soul, that's it.

The freedom you gave to me, I cannot get over. I don't want to get over it. I want to stay in it. I want to make a home in this freedom with you.

I want to feel this way for the rest of our lives. We may wake up to a completely altered world thriving in a whole new direction, if Jimmy is successful. Whatever possibly occurs, we can make it t together. We can make it happily ever after, if we try.

The vibes must have been right for you, or you wouldn't

even be here. Our souls intertwined that night. I've had my share of psychedelic experiences in my own time. The vibration we shared cannot be placed only on the trip.

Something special happened in that hammock. We both fell for each other. This is not the type of love that walks up to you every day. Feels like we may share a caring for each other that could last a lifetime.

I cannot ever possibly correctly express how great it felt to be free of my path here if only for a few hours. I really can't. This is how I know you have the power to help me slide into your era and finally feel comfortable. You feel comfortable with me too, I can tell.

My only goal now is to destroy the phone and completely be absorbed into a life into this era here with you. You've seen the phone and played with it. I'm ready for it to go away forever. I hope you are still down with the idea of me moving into these days quietly and seamlessly.

Starting my life here by your side is exactly what I want. I want to burn my old life with you. Let's start a new phase of our time here together. Please Rose take me by the hand and show me how to be a man of your time.

Take these crazy paranoid thoughts and help me turn them into relaxed peace and love filled expressions. You are why I came here; I didn't know it at the time. Now, I've never been this sure of anything. You can show me the way to be a completely different man.

The moment you put that phone down and cozied up with

me in that hammock it all went away. My past life, the Glowbox, all my worries were gone. I felt like the carefree king of the world till I woke up alone. You made it all disappear.

That was the first time since all this started, I literally forgot about all of it. It was beautiful and peaceful. It was the most serene moment I've had since this all happened. It was completely thanks to you.

Several hours of bliss and clarity of a hazy mind were amazing, to say the least. That night in the hammock I truly felt meshed into this era. I eased into become a man of this day and let all my past go. It was truly the moment I've been waiting for.

You gave me the one thing I truly wanted. You made me a part of these days. You made me experience a life lived in the sixties. My old life, for once, was not an all-consuming void.

From the time you put my phone down, until the time I woke up, I was in a state of literal ecstasy. Chasing you down was just as much about finding this source of bliss as it was getting my phone back. I wanted that feeling again. I want it every day.

I want that feeling for the rest of my life. A life with you is all I could've ever possibly wished for. We make one hell of a couple, and you know it too. Who knows what were capable of?

Love like this doesn't come around often. I don't plan on letting you go easily. We are two little peas in a trippy little pod. After all we've seen together, you can say we've got some history already.

If it's up to me, we'll take this energy we've created and run with it. It's up to you to show me around this beautiful age in our country's history. That's what's so crazy to me I still realize I'm slipping into history. To you it's just another day in the neighborhood.

To you I'm just some crazy abnormality that found its way into your life. It's just another day in the bay in 1968. It's a life full of concern for the war and your peers and the draft. Life is moving right along at its normal pace.

Myself, I'm finding my place in a pocket of time I've only fantasized about until I landed here. I spent plenty of lonely days here going to work and coming back to my little room. Trying to avoid as much social interaction as possible, in some attempt to keep any possible eyebrows from being raised.

I've lived so many indiscriminate vague days and nights here. I've hidden myself from this culture I'm obsessed with long enough. I cannot wait to tear this place wide open untethered to this insanity. I cannot wait to do it with you Rose.

Jimmy leaving with the Glowbox and burning this phone will be my ticket to a complete escape into the sixties. We can make a clean break into the haze. The surf and the beaches will call our names. My past will slowly become some weird glitch that is better left behind us.

Calling me Allen in a group will be the biggest everlasting hunk of weirdness. That's just the way the cookie crumbles. We got this. I can't believe it's finally over.

There's a chance for us to be happy people. I want to do that. Let's do that. I want to slide right into these days and never look back right by your side.

I want all this craziness to be our little secret and I want to get out and live. I'm tired of working and disappearing back into my little room. After work I want to climb into this van with you and hit the beach or the Haight. My dream is finally coming true thanks to you.

A spark was lit in me in that hammock I hope never goes out. I conceptualized leaving everything behind me for real. Now I want to bring that thought to reality. We can be happy here; I can be happy here.

I have no desire to curl back up in that meek existence I called a life before you came along. We can get out there and have a blast. Good music is being played every night here somewhere. An amazing revolution is alive all around us.

You can help me forget that I'm a traveler here from the future. That's a pretty remarkable power. Sneaking in and out of shows and never talking to anyone is over for this ole boy. I was so afraid to give myself away, I took being a fly on the wall to a new level.

Since the Glowbox is gone and my phone is soon to be out of existence, I will have no ties to the future and gladly leaving in the past. There will be no weird momentous secrets looming in the back of my mind constantly. This is the beginning of me finally living the life I've only dreamed of here. The life here I knew was possible.

There's going to be a lot of little weird moments I'll go ahead tell you just because of my past. We can handle it though. The longer time goes on it will just seek farther and farther into memories barely even reflected on. Those are the moments I can't wait for.

The longer our years go on together, the past of all this will be basically forgotten. This is what I absolutely cannot wait for. I become a man of these times, and those days are years behind me. We will be living a normal life and all that from before is just hazy memories.

The only real questions left on our minds will be about what happens if Jimmy is successful with the box. He could change the whole course of humanity in an instant. That's definitely some heavy stuff. Who knows what type of things can happen?

I hope he's successful and all three missions. Then, I hope he comes back here, and we can maybe plan another alteration. We have the power to change everything. I just hope the Night Foxes don't have a way to track if it's being used.

I've never used it since I came here. I even popped up in the middle of the woods on purpose in case they did track me. Then, I immediately high-tailed it down to the city as quickly as possible. I was hoping to just disappear. My goal was to just mesh right into the beautiful peace seeking peers you have here.

Now, I just hope more than anything to do this with you by side. A woman like you is like the finest diamond you can find or like hitting the lottery. Your heart is full of love, not wondering how your internet sites are doing. Your attitude is one of peace and mutual understanding for your fellow man.

I want a heart like that. I want to be devoted to spreading the easy-going deep-thinking thoughts you share with your friends. People in my day are very jaded on open heartedness. It just got so common mindfulness is basically out the window, and it's terrible.

These things I tell you hopefully make it obvious why I want to absorb into your day instead of spreading some message about mine. I'll tell you and jimmy whatever you guys want to know. I just don't wish to talk about it with anyone else.

Who knows what kind of insane set of events we would put into motion if we showed all kinds of people my phone and I would tell them tales of the future. I would rather destroy the phone and become a permanent fixture of this beautiful period of human history. We would never have a moment's peace if we shared what I know. The folks here are better off not knowing what's coming if you ask me.

There is a whole group of people from my day who still listen to the listen to the music from your time and have concerts and campouts that we believe touch on the vibration your generation produced. From what I've seen some of them come pretty close. There is a whole infectious way of life being created, which is glorious, but you are just trying to hang out and have fun. I assure you that the energy of revolution and peace and love you're trying to create does not ever die!

That energy accepted me and let me in that night in the

hammock. For the first time since I came here, I felt a part of this era, instead of a sneaky visitor. Holding you and feeling you in my arms somehow freed me. I fully accredit you and the energy you exchanged with me while we made love.

Connection like that had never enveloped me. I have had plenty of sex on acid at festivals in my day, but never felt completely unified like we did. I cannot simply write off the experience as good sex on acid. We melted into one entity, and we can do this for the rest of our lives.

Apparently, I wasn't alone in that thinking because here we are. You've seen Jimmy leave our reality. You've seen my phone and gave it back. I'm still sitting here with your hand in mine, we have something special.

We have love. Peace and love, isn't that the main idea your generation is trying to show to the public? Here we are, we've found it. It's up to us to keep it, to not just keep it but treasure it and protect it.

I completely forgot about the phone and the Glowbox. I forgot about all the craziness from my time. I was just a soul and a body in a hammock with an amazing woman and that's all I needed to be. Thanks to you that's all I need to be.

Regardless of the alien device you had just been playing with, your attraction superseded your curiosity, and we made the sweetest vibration one can ask for. I was beginning to think you were going to just play with that phone till at least the battery died. When you just sat it to the side and rolled over and kissed me, I was in awe. I really didn't expect it.

With such amazing technology in your hands, I figured any intention you had of being with me was out the window. It wasn't. I'll never be able to explain to you the surprise I felt when you were bored with the phone and got back to being alone in the hammock with me. You proceeded to give me the most special moment of my life.

Our souls must have stretched to the far corners of the universe. I have never felt so free and calm to be out of my body, but still together with you. Psychedelics are around in my day too, so I am certainly no stranger to them. I was as close to a hippy as a man can be in 2009.

Granted we had to either listen to the music over a stereo or from a band that plays a lot of the older songs which are just being written right now! I can now listen to the original songs being played live and that is nothing short of a miracle, I suppose. A miracle is something that is technically not supposed to happen.

A chance of unimaginable fate has led me here to you. I am going to get to see all these shows I watched on a screen in my time right in front of me with my arms around you. I'll never understand how I got so lucky; I'll never question it either. I will simply squeeze you tighter and give thanks and praise for somehow being here.

While I'm doing that, I'll give a thousand times more thanks and praise for being in the arms of your true love. Just let me know if I'm ever squeezing you too tight. Being here in this era is without a doubt amazing. Spending it with someone who wants me in her life more than anything is far more priceless.

Only the lucky ones get to spend their lives with a companion who truly adores and values them. The days I come from are severely lacking in healthy relationships. They are truly, truly few and far between. This technology I'm telling you about really destroys people's chances to be happy together.

The couples who do make it in my day don't typically spend a lot of time messing with their phones and tablets and the internet. There are so many people who don't give a crap if they tear apart a whole family just to trick someone into sleeping with them one time. Now, where do they meet these psychos...typically on the internet.

The days I'm from it's not strange at all for a mother or father to desert their whole family for some person they barely know from a website. Family units are nothing like what you think of from your time. Most families are not the same mother and father who started them. Parents being together for life is not very common where I come from.

Family statistics these days are basically the exact opposite of the time I'm from. Do most of your friends come from homes where both parents are still together? Sure, they do. Things change drastically over the years to come.

Divorces are not very common here. Parents go through more than we could ever imagine, keeping their families together, these days. Where I come from there isn't commitment like this. This leaves children in some precarious places.

People begin relationships with the same type of love as parents of this time. They have so many years together as happy people. When things get difficult, however, they just go their separate ways. There doesn't seem to be much effort to see each other through a difficult patch.

I'm sure there are couples all over this planet going through the same troubles people in my day go through. The only difference is these days they work through it. The internet just helps a person in a relationship start looking around to see what else is out there. Before you know it, like I told you, one parent is asking for divorce and taking off with a stranger they've met online.

I don't think a woman should stay in a home where she's getting beat on. A person should not stay in a home where the children are subjected to trauma after trauma just for the sake of keeping a family together don't get me wrong. A happy, healthy home should be the ultimate goal for your children.

This is not even important in my time. Once, a person in the couple has decided they can do better they typically pursue that completely behind their partner's back. They usually do this with these phones and computers on what I'm teaching you about is called the internet. It seems to me they don't give much effort into fixing the home they've made and communicating where they're becoming unhappy.

One thing I hope we always do is talk to each other if we are having problems with some behavior. I want the whole deal with you. We could be two old hippies sitting on our front porch swing griping at our kids for the crazy stuff they are doing. The same way your parents give you a hard time going to all these rocks shows.

If they only had one clue, you were seeing some of the most famous musicians to ever live. They don't and never will, to them it's just loud pot-smoking music. These bands changed history and I want to catch every second of it we can. I know how precious these days and bands are.

We are in the epicenter of possibly the biggest musical revolution ever. You have a van and I have a decent job, which means I have got some money, and you have a ride we can sleep in. We can catch so many shows that are replayed and studied in my time. We will be right up in the middle of the best music ever played.

These are the days you grew up in. You don't think it's such a bid deal to catch Janis Joplin and The Grateful Dead on the weekend because you're bored. In my days, these artists are known as beyond legends. Their music is regarded as timeless.

Hopefully, that helps you understand why I'm so excited to see them live. I've only watched countless hours of footage from their live shows and listened to the albums. We can see them play live all the time. Words cannot express how happy I am to go to these concerts.

I went to some shows by myself since I've been here. I told you I never really talked to anyone and just crept back into the shadows when it was over. Dancing and singing with you will be a completely different experience. Stretching out on a blanket with you while this amazing piece of American history plays out around us is indescribable.

We both fell in love that night in the woods. A cellphone in your hands in 1968 most've been like holding an alien's laser gun. I'll never forget the look in your face when you put it down and rolled over on top of me. The fact that being alone with me was more interesting than that phone confirmed to me that I was more than just company in the woods at least.

Our spirits shared a space that night. While our bodies were doing whatever dirty things they were down there doing, our souls were connecting on a level we may never understand. I'm not even going to try to make sense of it. I'm just doing my best to hold your little hand until you want me to stop, which hopefully is never!

The look on your face when I surprised you at your house with Chuckie was fear at first, because you knew why I was there. Then I saw happiness in your eyes to see me again. Right then, I knew it was not just me who caught feelings in the woods the night before. Thank God!

I cannot tell you enough, I was more worried about trying to keep you in my life than that stupid freaking phone. A woman like you is a true gem. The way it feels when you touch my skin can only be described by words like bliss or Heaven. That's the thing I really came barreling out of those misty woods for the second I opened my eyes.

The phone had to be retrieved, of course, I never had any intentions of it being exposed to the public. I knew finding the phone meant finding you. Once you were found I would have a chance to ask if you felt the same. You do, and Good Lord I'm a lucky man because of it.

The destruction of that darn thing will be a sense of relief for me I cannot explain. I would be a liar if I said I hadn't toyed with the idea of making some kind of fortune from it. Seemed like any avenue I would go down to try and sell it would end me up in some secret place with the military asking a trillion questions and possibly making me disappear again, but for good this time. Seeing it disappear into a clump of melting black plastic and hiding any possible leftover fragments seems like the safest bet.

It can no longer be a black cloud lurking over my shoulder once it's gone. You couldn't help but take it and run with it, even after the incredible night we shared. So, you know firsthand understand the power it possesses. It's gotta go!

Our charisma is worth everything in the world. The way it felt in that hammock can go on forever. We have an amazing vibe together. I believe we may possibly have a chance to make it.

To me having love by your side is worth more than anything money could ever buy. I'm not getting down one knee and proposing, yet. I'm just asking if we can hit some shows together and spend some time by each other's side and see if we have real magic between us or if the hammock was just some kind of fluke. I don't believe it was, do you?

Chapter 8: Mystical Mountain Hop

When I opened my eyes and realized you were gone with the phone, I believe my brain reset. At first, I tried to justify it. Trying to tell myself you were just gone getting coffee rather than you had just completely ditched me in the middle of nowhere, and you were loose in 1968 with a touchscreen phone was stupid. That didn't last long.

I got up quick and packed up everything. Camping on my way back down to the city was my only option, it seemed. Admitting I was shocked is an understatement. It seemed like you were enjoying yourself that night. I did not expect you to jet.

Running into Chuckie as soon as I hit town was not even on my list of possibilities. Do you know how far it is from the middle of the woods back to that little town? It's about 5 miles. I know that cause you made me walk exactly that when you took off. Not cool.

I had a lot of time to think about my current situation. It

didn't take me long to admit to myself that I just wanted to be back around you. The woods were so beautiful that morning. The fog looked like smoke rolling in every direction; it was so thick.

Walking down that trail was incredible. I still had my afterglow going on from us tripping. I love the next day; you feel so clean and light. It's the opposite of a hangover; you don't feel bad; you feel better.

Marching through those mist-filled woods with the morning sun peeking through was gorgeous. There were still two beers left, so I just sipped on those walking my happy ass out of there thinking about you. I had to get my phone back ASAP, of course, but I got my wish because you stayed with me.

This part of California is just so beautiful. It was still trippy walking through all that mist, it was so thick. There were times I couldn't see more than six inches in front of me. It was a pleasant experience.

I had never been here until I used the Glowbox. I had never been farther than Alabama. It's grown on me. I couldn't imagine living anywhere else now. I certainly wouldn't want to.

The biggest thing I was concerned with was getting with you. I had no idea how to find you. I was so worried. I was running all these worst-case scenarios through my head while walking. Picturing myself going from beach to beach trying to find you, or you taking it right to the police had me scared to death.

I kept picturing a bunch of cops rolling up on me the entire time until I found you. You left me so paranoid. There was no possible way for me to know what you were possibly doing with it. The woods were just waking up, and all the nature was just starting the normal morning routine. Focusing on that was the best way for me to try to keep my mind off you.

The more I walked, the sunbeams kept warming up the morning mist, sending it up to join the clouds. It was completely gone before I hit town. It was just your typical beautiful, sunny morning by the time I made it to the diner. Watching all the fog go up into the sky was nice.

My poor brain was jumping like a frog, but I tried to stay focused on how glorious the walk was. I was terrified deep down. I had no idea how to track you down or what you were doing with the phone. It was a lot to take in.

The first time I tried to open up about what had happened, I was ditched in the woods, and my phone was floating around 1968. I felt so stupid. The fact that only you, your mom, and Chuckie saw it was such a relief.

On my way out of those woods, I replayed my whole life in my head. Comparing my time to yours kept repeating over and over. I had only heard stories and watched videos of these days. I'm happy here.

Since I found you so easy and damage control was minimal, I feel a lot better about everything. I was ecstatic compared to all the possible outcomes that played through my head. The fact that you stayed with me is priceless. Where do I begin to explain?

I got to rethink every moment of my existence through my hazy brain. I saw my time here being so peaceful. When I compared it to the age I came from, I knew I never wanted to go home. I had no desire whatsoever.

The fact that I was away from the technology-driven period I was from was such a pleasant thought. Flashing back and forth from my days to these was a recurring theme. I used to check my phone two hundred times a day. No exaggeration.

The people from my period spend so much time staring at a screen it's hard to put it into words. Most folks in my day typically spend a large percentage of their day on some form of electric device. There's absolutely nothing like it to compare to here, which is a good thing. You and all your friends are truly connected, and it's awesome.

Almost everyone in my day spends more time looking at a device than the beautiful planet they're living on. It's commonplace. I thought a lot about my old life. I had a nice walk out of the woods.

The way of life here really jumped out at me. I love it here. The protest rallies are insane. I have no desire to return to my old days.

The people here actually listen to each other. The people where I'm from all just sit together while they all simultaneously do their own thing on some type of device. They are typically really distracted. The genuine conversation you guys have here is so priceless.

I just trudged on through the woods, thinking all spacey,

and I just knew in my gut that it would all be okay. All those thoughts of something terrible coming from you having it was just paranoia, I told myself. I just hoped I was right.

Given the situation, if I were you, I would've run off with the phone from the future too. Waiting till the morning would've been a way better plan. I truly should have waited till after we woke up to show it to you. It's all good though.

My good karma kicked in, and ole Chuckie brought me right to you. I could hardly believe my eyes when I saw him walking across the parking lot. I had no idea he knew where to find you. That was such a blessing.

I had imagined looking for weeks. I had no idea how to even begin to find you. The elation I felt when he said he knew where to find you was incredible. The only way to describe it is like a million tons of weight coming off my chest. I wouldn't have to do all the hopeless searching while you were loose with the phone.

My happiness at finding the phone so fast was overshadowed entirely by seeing you and hopefully us hanging out together. There's no way I was more worried about the phone than you. Once the phone is destroyed, I can truly feel free. It's going to be amazing.

My primary goal is to stay with you, by your side. You're the coolest woman I've ever met. We are going to make one badass couple. I mean, you just saw a guy time travel and then just continued to hang out.

These days, they are crazy in their own way. You know, all

the protesting and energy is beyond words for me. I promise there are still many forms of protest and outcrying of people in the future. Unfortunately, a large majority turn violent.

I was still a little spacey, so staring into the mist left me replaying old memories from the future. I kept going back to how folks from my day all spend their time staring into their device. I'm so enthralled by how you guys engage in a collective conversation. I love it.

Weird, static-charged memories of you kept twisting their way through my mystical, nostalgic five-mile march. The future isn't all bad. People are just far more independent. They don't spend nearly as much time just hanging out in a big group like your generation.

It's really a shame. More than all the historical events that occurred between now and my time, I was stuck on the difference in social interactions. Whereas you guys may try a home phone before you just jump in your vehicle and go where you think people are, which is awesome. Most people in my day look at their phones to see where people are, if they even go out.

Disposing of this phone is going to be so great. It's going to be amazing to have one less thing to worry about. You have no idea. I've had the worst thoughts of terrible scenarios that could've played out if I got caught with it.

My biggest conclusion is that I would much rather spend my life here. Life is so much simpler. I could even take you to the future when Jimmy gets back. You must promise that we will come back here afterward.

I'm not going to say too much about my day. You need to experience it for yourself. I don't want to make you feel jaded like me. There could be a completely different experience. Who knows what Jimmy will accomplish?

My little walk through my foggy memories on my way back to town left me feeling really nostalgic. The way things used to be for me in the future may be a completely different journey. Jimmy may reshape the course of humanity for both of us. The future I could tell you too much about may not even happen.

Making myself focus on the beauty of the vapors evaporating into the morning light was the best thing I could've ever done. The scenery blended perfectly with my hazy mindset. I compared my time here with the humanity I had known quite a bit.

There was no way I could ever go back to the buzzing, ringing beehive I was used to after spending time here; that was for certain. You are an amazing, fearless girl. I want to spend my days here. I want to spend it with you.

It's a curious thought to take you to the current time I'm from. Everything may become instantly different, if Jimmy is successful for just one mission. You could possibly be going to a completely different dimension, one that's literally brand new. This is very exciting.

Heroes... is the way our story may play out. Jimmy and I are now certainly time pirates. You're probably going to be next. I don't see us really discarding it once he gets back.

It's impossible to not get lost in the possibilities that can arise from a completed mission by Jimmy. Anything could happen. I worry about backfires. There is a chance that him saving one of these people could drastically shift humanity in a negative way.

Those possibilities circulate a lot in my thought patterns. I'm trying not to get stuck on them. There will be no way of knowing until he gets back. One thing is for sure, he's gone.

He's out there trying to literally change the world. We can only hope and wait. Where and when would you like to go with it when he gets back? We can't dangle a time machine in front of you and not give you a chance to use it.

We could even go way farther into the future. There's no limit to where we go. My biggest fear is the fact that we don't know anything about the culture there. There's no way we can predict what they wear or how they act.

It could be a catastrophic failure if we immediately draw attention to ourselves upon arrival. We have no idea what their form of currency is. I have a lot of apprehension about going further into time. I would be a liar if I said the thought had never crossed my mind.

I'm not sure how we could truly prepare for such an expedition. It would be incredible to see one hundred years ahead. Do we truly want to even know what's to come? If Jimmy accomplishes just one goal everything will be drastically different already, I believe.

So, now here's the big question... Do we even want to use

the thing again once he gets back? I can't be sure my answer is yes. We may want to just dispose of it somehow and be done with all this madness. There's really no way of knowing what kind of residual physical effects I'll be left with from using it.

I may grow out the back of my head the size of a basketball. I don't know. Honestly, I'm still not completely sure how the Glowbox even works. There's a way of telling what kind of crazy frequencies you're exposed to when you use it.

So far, so good. That's the best I can say at this point. We'll use it if you wish us to. That's how much I love you. I can't tell you the final results with any certainty, though.

I can tell you that I wish to spend most of our lives right here in the sixties. There's a simplicity to life in this era that is so intoxicating now that I'm used to it. I want to destroy the phone immediately, regardless. When Jimmy gets back, we can discuss further use of the Glowbox.

Right now, I just need you to understand your era is amazing. It's one of the most famous periods in human history and we should appreciate getting to live it. There are things happening right now that are a huge part of the way American culture plays out. You grew up here so this all feels so normal to you.

I want to spend the rest of my days here. I can't be more direct about that. I guess I kind of hope you choose not to use it. I'm with you either way it goes.

Deep down beside you is where I want to be. I want to get lost in this psychedelic circus you call the Bay Area and live a life I've only dreamed of a million times. I've seen what's to come for many years. I want to live my life right here, right now.

I could tell you reason after reason why. Jimmy may change the flow of everything I came to accept as reality, so I truly don't want to say too much. I just want you to know we are right in the middle of one of the most important times in American history, and I want to get lost in it with you. I don't want to go back.

Chapter 9: Words Cannot Express

Déjà vu means already seen in French. The fact that I've felt this moment (in the past) truly messes with me. Words cannot describe the deep level of connectivity I have with our time here today in this van. What if we tap into our timelines our whole lives?

Do you think Jimmy will really change humanity? I hope he does. You know I didn't plan on any of this. There wasn't a bit of premeditated thought put into the moment that has led us to this point. I could never deny I've felt this for basically all my life, though, sweetie. All of this came to fruition because I was on the run.

You are taking this all like a champ. I know me coming into your life is like trying to get comfortable beside a hurricane. Trust me. Take it from the hurricane. I keep trying to put myself in your shoes, I can't, though.

We just saw a man travel back in time. This is so hard to fathom. Even though I have done it twice. The sight was incredible none-the-less. Rose looking into the sunset with you is a welcome sun-soaked end to that chapter. Watching this beautiful California sky was never on my radar when I was just a lonely, bored boy trying to earn a military pension.

I will be honest, I wanted to get rid of the Glowbox long before we met. Now that we are together, it is a no-brainer. I just want to live the rest of my days here in Paisley-covered bliss with you if possible.

I chose to come to Frisco in the sixties. I lucked into spending it with you. We are like two sweet little peas in a pod. True connection is rare in any place. Real love is surely not to be taken lightly.

I came here for peace and love, so show me some love, pretty lady. I want you to tell me everything you can about growing up in these times. I want to forget about growing up amongst all the turmoil I witnessed in the nineties. It's not possible.

I wish I could show you Tupac and the Bush administration and all these crazy things to come, but I won't. I guess I don't even want you to see the future. You can, however, take me deep into a time people of my age only fantasize about. Thank God for that.

You said you and your brother used to go to the park and watch the bands play for free. I could not imagine watching Jefferson Airplane play on a Friday night for free cause there was nothing else to do. People from my generation watch videos of them performing like it's a class in college. Those things are now my reality.

I grew up in an era engulfed in street gang violence. Serious turbulence arises amongst folks just trying to survive. They were all so self-absorbed. The people had a sense of life versus death you won't understand.

You don't have to worry about some gun-crazed kid killing you for a pair of red shoes. I don't know how to tell you that is what this city is in for, this town becomes a mecca of gang activity. The whole state of California becomes plagued by these gangs. Californians pay a serious price due to their murderous ways.

The days I grew up in compared to these days are treacherous at best. Words cannot express how happy I am to be Robert now, and to be here with you. There will come a point when I vaguely remember those times. They can't come soon enough.

I want to get into the vibrations you guys feel. Forgetting the frantic survival mentality we all grew accustomed to sounds amazing. Trust me, love, if you knew what I knew, you would want the same. I don't want you to know.

That's what I love about your era...you don't even know what a gang banger is. They are serial killers in my time. They kill people for what seems to most of us for no reason at all. Murders of men, women, and children are rampant. The deaths result from really no cause at all, other than being at the wrong place at the wrong time.

They say it's because of territory and/or respect. The easiest message that can be conveyed comes down to wearing different colors, because it gives them a reason to attack. Retaliation is the root factor. Seeking vengeance for a fallen comrade leaves the killing of anyone wearing the wrong color.

This makes absolutely no sense to me, red and blue and yellow and whatever colors you can think of, they wear it like a uniform. I'm guessing it will make no sense to you. I'm just trying to describe the future to you. They are like roving gangs of violent outlaws who all wear the same color.

Tupac was a gang banger. He made good rap music. He was true to his roots, which were deep in the Black Panther movement because of his mom. His lyrics blatantly stated a hatred for white people.

Rap music is a kind of poetry set to music. Most of the time, the artists are black people, and the music is typically made electronically. It's created with computers and not with a band. That's really nothing like it in your day.

Back here, it's all so organic and electric. The music and vibration of my time are all so calculated. It all sounds like a robot made it. I can't describe to you how amazing it is to absorb your culture.

Words really cannot convey the joy I feel in getting to soak up your time period. There is adversity here for free thinkers, of course. My day, sweetie, is full of constant invasion of peace of mind. It's a scary thing.

You guys are free to lay in the grass and stretch out your legs and soak up the sky and bless you for it. The energy your generation set free is part of what fuels the nearly empty tanks of the free thinkers of my day. I can't describe to you enough how hard people of my day cling to some of your principles. The attitudes about the policy your generation is trying to put in place are amazing.

I want to fall into this time with you like a stranger with a purpose and a road map to the high points. It's scary to think that I know a little bit about what's to come, but so be it. I guess we can say I've got an inside track on things to come. I'm not even mad about you ditching me to steal the phone. I promise.

We need to soak this up. I need to soak this up. I know you're bored with all this tie-die and whatever comes with it, but darling, if you were looking back from where I am, you would see the true beauty like I do. I know it seems like I have nothing good to say about the future.

There's not a lot of high points to illustrate barring technological advancements.

I have only stern lessons to give you and that is quite a bummer. Unfortunately, that is how reality is going to pan out. Maybe ole Jimmy will pull it out for us.

He may possibly create some change that we wake up to and the world will have transformed. Hopefully, it will have morphed into some gorgeous utopia as opposed to the dystopia my generation grew up in. I guess we can only hope. For now, this is what we have.

A new day may not come for us. You can decide to leave me right now and if you do all I can say is do not take this time for granted. There is an energy in the air that becomes harder and harder to grab hold of. So, please don't take advantage of these days you're lucky enough to grow up in.

You are so beautiful you have your pick of men. I know how lucky I am to be the one you have by your side. You are so fun. I'm having a blast.

When I first traveled from my day and accidentally ended up in the 50s, I was lost. I spent a couple of nights in the woods, putting thoughts into what had just happened. Having read the instructions for the Glowbox was the only reason there was even comprehension of what happened. Slipping back into my old life was really what was planned.

All I can do is express to you the beauty of the day you live in. I chose to come here out of any place in time and space and you were lucky to have been placed here by the universe. I hope you don't squander it. More than that I hope you let me share it with you.

Imagine if he does save Martin Luther King Jr. and the black movement gets that much more powerful and the gangs don't get so much foothold in the hearts of the youth. What if he killed Hitler and millions of people weren't killed in the insanity? I can't even try to relate some of these emotions.

What if we wake up to a whole new era of humanity one day and it will all seem natural because the timeline has changed seamlessly? This is why I gave the box to Jimmy instead of just trashing it and disposing of it in the ocean. There's hope for a completely different human race in my heart.

We saw him leave. We have possibly set into motion a complete change in human history. I just truly hope somehow it doesn't backfire. Deep down, I'm terrified he will put a tragic ripple effect in play that causes damage to life as we know it. This is a risk I'm willing to take, but geez, I'm scared to death of possible negative effects.

This is a chance I had to take. Especially after the stuff I've told you about how the future pans out. I'm just praying Jimmy will be able to talk MLK into taking his security more seriously and not taking that trip to Memphis.

He was a leader of peace and so was JFK. We both know it would nearly be impossible for him to get a message across to a president. However, just imagine if he did and the Kennedys got to continue their roles by disbanding organized crime's grip on politicians. My mind could do this all day, you know, correcting scenarios that played out bad for mankind.

Just imagine if for example, Jim Morrison, Janis Joplin, and Jimi Hendrix didn't die untimely deaths... along with countless others. The impact that would've made on music is astronomical. The same principle can be applied to any other area of life. Time and change are the only real constants.

Jimmy chose to focus on preventing King's death first. He decided on this even more so after our talk about what I saw in the future. If you could go anywhere in human history, where would you go? Would you go forward or backward if the Glowbox was yours?

The hard part about using the box is being ready to blend in with the era you're going to. Slang and, appearance and images change so much. Jimmy is ready for that. That's obvious.

His experience as a history teacher gives me hope he'll be able to adapt. This is a scary conversation. Changing the course of human history is a tricky business. Do you think he'll pull it off? I sure hope so.

Chapter 10: Ready to Die for It

It was a long, cold walk in the rain back to Crescent City from the woods. You didn't even think about liking me on your drive back south? Did you? It was surely fate for me to find you. Do you believe in that kind of thing, sweetie?

When I made it back to Crescent City, the first person I really saw was Chuckie! I lied to him. I said that I'd left my wallet in your van. I knew he would surely take me back to you that way.

I hated to lie to him, but it's not like I could tell him you stole my device from the future. It was so hard to hide my true frantic energy and just act casually. My mind was spinning a million miles a minute. I didn't know if you had taken it to the cops. I was worried.

I asked him to wait in his car, because I really didn't want him to see the phone. The whole car ride back down to San Francisco I was a nervous wreck. I was running all these scenarios through my head.

I was terrified to think maybe you had taken it straight to the police. My head was swimming, honestly. I was already in love with your energy. The fact that you had stolen my phone was already secondary.

I walked into a cafe on the edge of town, soaking wet and shivering. I was so paranoid the police were about to come grab me up before I even made it off that country road. I sat down in this cafe trying to wrangle up a cup of coffee just to warm up. I'll never forget the level of fear coursing through me. I looked out the window and by the grace of the good Lord above, Chuckie had just pulled up at the surf shop across the street.

I ran straight out of the restaurant and almost forgot to throw some change on the table for the coffee. I didn't even wait for the coffee to come. The waitress was trying to get my attention while I was running out of the door, I just blurted out "It's on the table." I'm sure I looked like a madman running across the street yelling at Chuckie and waving my arms. The look on his face before he recognized who was running across the street screaming his name proved that fact.

It was just my luck he was just about to drop his surfboard off and head back down to Frisco. Thank God he smoked a joint with me on the way back to town. My heart was beating out of my chest worrying about what you'd done with the phone.

I hated to do it, because he's such a sweetheart. I had to lie to him about why I needed to get to you. I told him you had left me there on purpose.

I told him I was visiting friends and you had to get back to town in a hurry, it was best I could do in a pinch trying to explain my circumstance. He was so happy that I really liked you that he was beside himself. He kept going on about what an awesome couple we would make. I think he's right.

We got pulled over by the police when we were halfway back because of his swerving. I got to try out my fake driver's license and it worked. I'm glad he hadn't lit the joint behind his ear up already when the cops got us. As soon as they pulled away, he goes "You want to smoke one?"

Considering I just had to use my fake identity on California Highway Patrol, and you were on the loose with my cell phone in the sixties of course, I took him up on it. He had a joint behind his ear the whole time the cops were talking to us, you just couldn't see it because of his hair! He already had a bag in the trunk of his Malibu, he pulled it off.

By the time we made it to you I had already secured the smoke I needed to hopefully talk Jimmy into taking the machine. So, I only had two goals left: becoming your man and getting the phone back. I've got the phone. How do you feel about staying together?

I didn't even think you would be at your mom's. However, if he took me there, I would have a home base in my search for you and my phone. That was one long and anxious ride down the coast! I cannot convey to you enough how much my anger for you was over-shadowed by this genuine shine I had taken to you.

I'm a lucky man since apparently you feel it too. True love like ours doesn't happen every day, sadly enough, some people go their entire lives and never feel it at all. What we have is truly special, and you know it. If you didn't, we wouldn't be here.

We've given Jimmy the Glowbox and truly can start a life together. I'll just have to get used to being called Robert. This alias stuff is for the birds. If we accidentally slip and you use my real name, we'll just say my middle name is Allen.

I guess I would rather you call me that when we're alone. I'll never get used to the alias, call me Allen whenever you want. I know I'm asking a lot of you to call me Allen when we're alone and Robert around strangers. Trust me.

I just hope I still have a chance with you and apparently, you're going to cause here we are. I want to get on your laid-back sixties mentality far more than I want to bring you to my uptight 21st-century attitude. Just show me around like I'm new here. Explain everything to me like I'm a foreigner because I really am. The times I grew up in are nothing at all like the times you're living in now.

Jimmy told you his plan for saving MLK, but he did not get into detail about how he's going to kill Hitler. I'm not sure if he told you that he's fluent in German. He's convinced, with his knowledge of history and the German language, that he can kill Hitler. He's ready to die for it too.

The night we talked about it in detail, he said that if he killed Hitler with his last breath, then it would be worth it. I must agree. He's ready to just shoot him as he walks by and die from shots from his guards on the spot, if that's the only way.

I have to say more power to him. Can you really imagine if the holocaust never happened? An entire World War could possibly be avoided. Millions upon millions of lives would be saved.

This could happen all because some hippy got ahold of a time machine and had the nerve to die for what he believed in. He's a real hero if you ask me. Jimmy's plummeting into the unknown. Who knows what awaits him?

I was selfish with my use of the Glowbox. Jimmy is ready to sacrifice his life in conjunction with having access to the box. Just because he can use it, he's ready to die to save the lives of millions and all I did was try to catch some Grateful Dead concerts in Golden Gate Park. He we are now, however.

I must ask you if you think I'm selfish. I used the Glowbox to sneak off and become a hippy and he used it to try and save the world. Rose, does that make me selfish? I seriously want your input.

This has been a big issue on my mind since I gave Jimmy the Glowbox. I feel like I'm being selfish. I hope to God he changes the course of human history. I just used it to go to my favorite time in American history.

Chapter 11: The Dead in a Flatbed

I'll never forget the look on your face when you saw me walk into your mom's backyard. I'm not sure what you thought you were going to even do with the phone. I'm sure you didn't even really have a plan. Your fight or flight response just told you to take the phone and run right.

I bet you didn't think I could find my way to your house, but I did! I'm so glad I did, too. I'm glad not just because I got the phone back, but mostly because now we're back together and you are the coolest girl I've ever met. I really want to try to stay together, sweetie.

The look on Chuckie's face when he saw my cell phone was just priceless. Chuckie, seeing it was a definite detour you created. I only wanted you to see the phone. The only reason I even wanted to show it to you was so that you could understand me. I already knew I had a thing for you.

I never intended for him to know any of this; however, it's too late now. I'm going to have to hide the phone somewhere else, because you know Chuckie's going to tell a couple of people what he saw. We're going to have to really talk our way out of this one somehow. I would talk about it eventually, if I was in his shoes.

Seems like Chuckie and your mom are both awesome people. They hopefully can keep my secret and just keep what they've seen to themselves. This is the part I've always been terrified about; you know. Showing someone an object that isn't invented for decades to come is dangerous ground.

Say one of them decides the best thing they could do is tell everyone they meet about what they've seen. That could be catastrophic. If I'm lucky, whoever they tell will think they're crazy as a loon. If I'm not, then I'm in big trouble.

This is the era I chose though, so all this is just background noise I must come to terms with. I only let you see the phone because I really fell for. Your mom and Chuckie knowing about this makes me a nervous wreck. It really does.

It's too late now, we'll have to go with it. There's no other choice. I've done well, though, in my opinion. I've been here a while now and you three are the only ones to know my secret. It's a big, weird secret, though.

If you choose to stay with me then you three will be the only ones that will ever have to know. Well, I guess when Jimmy comes back then that'll make four. Do you think you can hang out with me a little longer after all this craziness? I sure hope so.

More than anything I've ever imagined, I want to live my

life here with you. I won't have to keep up some crazy lie with your mom if we're going to be together. I hate lying. I really want you to be the one to show me around the sixties and the bay area for the rest of my life.

You're the most gorgeous, intelligent, and fun-loving woman I could've asked for. I'm a lucky man to be the one by your side. We make a good couple. Spending my time here with you would be an absolute blessing.

Please show me how to live a life based on peace and love and not fear and selfishness. People of my time don't usually think much about that. Most are seriously consumed with self-committed goals. They pay little attention to the effect they have on the world.

Typically, people are alone in a room with five people when they are all where I'm from. Each person is engulfed in their device and hardly a word is spoken. I want to get more into the way you guys interact, you completely conversate. We don't.

Do you think Jimmy will ever come back here? I wonder if we'll ever see him again. Let's say he achieves his mission and stops these catastrophes. I'm rooting for him.

We will never know. The whole world will just be different in the blink of an eye. Things will just be different, and I guess no one will ever know the difference.

These people will do completely different things and the whole path of history will be an absolute parallel with what we know! That's very powerful stuff. I must admit this is the draw of the Glowbox that kept me from destroying it. I've often imagined the possible outcomes from successful uses of it.

I've feared the possible tragic outcomes of using it, as well. This is why I've almost destroyed it many times. I was just sitting in the sand at Bolinas Beach with the Glowbox and controller, waiting on a rental boat when I met Chuckie. I was going to drop it in the bay.

The bottom of the ocean seemed like the best place to me for the Glowbox at that point. I had gotten a metal lock box it would fit in and packed it down there to the beach, in a backpack. A boat was reserved for the purpose of dumping the Glowbox in the bay. I was sitting by the dock of the bay, obviously looking distraught when Chuckie walked up to me.

Honestly, if Chuckie hadn't struck up a conversation, I probably would've dropped it in the water that day. He looked down at me and said, "Rough day, buddy?" I covered my eyes to shield them from the sun he was standing in when I looked up and noticed a big joint behind his ear. I replied, "Might not be as bad if you decided to share that doobie."

He laughed and lit it up, now, he we are. Let's hope the right choice was made. We won't know until Jimmy either dies or completes his missions. Let's keep our fingers crossed.

Meeting Chuckie that day was the true catalyst for lots of things in my life. He got me so stoned I changed my mind about the boat that day, at least. Suddenly then, it seemed way too much work. He took me home and sold me some of his pot.

He kept asking what was in the backpack. He couldn't get over how I never said what was in it. He kept saying, "What is it? A head." he knows now.

A short time later, we watched Jimmy travel back in time and I'm completely in love. I am totally down to let you show me around this place. We can go over to Haight and Ashbury and watch this Dead show. We can do it knowing we may have set in place the most positive changes the world will ever know, or not know. This is incredible, my sweet little Rosie girl.

That's what I hope for. I want you to disappear with me into the love of your era and help me shake off all this '90s craziness. How does that sound? Could you help me blend into your day?

I heard the Grateful Dead are playing in the back of a flatbed truck on Haight Street tonight for free. We could, at least, go to that. It would be awesome to go camping in the woods by that Crescent City beach after it's over. That sounds good to me, at least.

Chapter 12: Sacrifice

I'm so glad I rode there to your mom's place with Chuckie. That way we could smoke some pot and relax while I talked to you guys about the phone. I only planned on showing you alone the evidence of my jumping time. I had no intention, whatsoever, of your mom and Chuckie seeing it.

It seems to me that your mom and Chuckie took it well, though. Hopefully, you four will be the only ones I have to walk all this through this. It was strange, to say the least. I truly was showing you an object from the future, which was very surreal.

I honestly felt like some kind of alien when I was just sitting there watching you guys flip through the phone. The only thing that could ever possibly feel the way I did would be an alien. Showing someone an item, they could have never imagined is truly interesting, to say the least.

I was just kicking back, smoking that joint and watching your eyes all just gleam with amazement. That honestly made me want you that much more. It made me think about how much I want to keep putting that look on your face for the rest of our lives. I'm not kidding.

I know you were just amazed by the phone. However, the way you looked up at me with those child's eyes and that beautiful, amazed, ear-to-ear smile will stay with me forever. It was hard to stay focused on showing you guys the phone while I was busy falling in love with you. I'm sure it was obvious I was distracted.

There's no way to deny how hard I've fallen for you. We can run through these beautiful days hand in hand completely in love and be lucky to do it. True love is rare. Fake love is everywhere.

I'm really glad your mom didn't run me out of the house at gunpoint and call the police. She surely was within her rights to do so. I guess she likes me, since she didn't. That`s a start, at least your mama can stand me.

You guys looked like kindergartners coloring with markers for the first time. You would think I had just shown you fire. The look of amazement in your faces from the glowing light of the screen was epic. I'm sure you guys were in some sort of shock.

I can only imagine it from your perspective. You guys are just happily cruising along and then some guy pops up with technology your minds hadn't even fathomed yet. I only showed it to you so you would know I'm not full of shit. You stealing it was not even on my radar.

You guys are now left with this big secret you have to keep for me. I'm sorry. You must help me hide this, Rose. I don't want anyone else to know.

Expose me and bring a huge wave of craziness into all our lives. I'm glad it's out in the open, though, honestly. I really am. We can discuss it freely and I don't have this enormous skeleton whispering to me from in my closet, which is very nice.

Keep in mind please the only reason I sprung this on you is because I'm in love with you. Your mom and Chuckie are just going along for the ride now, because you stole my phone. Here we are now, though. I want to spend my time here with you.

I've been here for years without you. Having felt the difference of you in my life, I truly wish for us to stay together. I had some lonely days here without you. I could sure use some time spent in your company.

Should we just throw the phone in the ocean? I just want to spend my days with you here. I don't want this awkward piece of my past to further affect my future with you. I really don't.

I just get paranoid that someone else will stumble upon it. I'm scared one of you guys will tell someone about it. Disposing of the phone would be a big relief to me. You can understand that.

I really don't care if we all get together and you guys play with the phone. I know it's an amazing phenomenon to you all. However, it's just a thorn in my side. This phone is just a danger hanging over my head.

I truly want to just destroy it. I just wish to disappear into the sixties forever. You make the call. That's how much power I'm giving you.

It's completely up to you, Rose if I destroy the darn thing or keep it. I would be happy burning it and then crushing it. I would like to bury the small, charred pieces deep in a hole way back in the woods. I'd like to cover that hole with a huge log, just in hopes there's no chance for anyone to stumble upon it.

It truly makes me nervous knowing it's here. If one of you guys decides to expose me for it, I can't even imagine the chaos that would ensue. I really can't. I try not to.

Since Jimmy is gone with the box my coveralls, my wallet, and phone are the only evidence left. I would really feel better destroying them just to be safe. Rather safe than sorry, right. I told you what I want to do with them.

I'm not sure what to do with this stuff, in all honesty. I really value your input here, sweetie. You've seen it and you know I'm not full of crap. I totally just want to destroy it.

I swear to God, I could rest then. That way I can finally really feel at peace here. I won't have this weird little plastic monkey on my back. It's always in the back of my mind.

I've even been thinking of going and hiding it somewhere that only I know about. That way if you want to play with it for a while, I can go get it and let you see it. That leaves us open to getting caught with it. What if a cop found it during a traffic stop?

I don't know why I'm giving you this much power in the situation. I guess it's just because this has got to be neat for you to use, I've thought of keeping it. Is a futuristic toy for you a good enough reason for me to stay a nervous wreck? Please say no.

I see the destruction and burial of the phone as almost a ceremonial gesture to my love for you. I see it as a means of leaving all the craziness behind and truly slipping into the sixties with you. Does that sound good to you my sweet little Rosie? I hope so.

I want nothing more than to just slide into this reality, with you, attachment free. This phone looming around seems to be the major hindrance to that. I say we go buy a gallon of gas, a hammer, and a shovel. Then we should go back to the spot where I first showed you the phone back in the woods.

I want to burn it, crush it, demolish it in every way and then bury it. After that, let's hide it under a bunch of trees and brush that shouldn't be disturbed for a very long time. I cannot explain to you the sense of peace I'll get from that. You have no idea.

Throwing it in the ocean means there's a chance of it being found. That's why I want to bury it where the elements will finish it off over the years. I wish to leave the smallest possible traces of it. Can you understand that?

Let's call that our next move. Head back to the woods tonight and help me literally bury my past. I can't think of anything that would make me happier other than staying with you, Rose.

We have fun together, and you know it. Let's do this. Let's sneak back off to the place where I fell in love with you. Let me leave this stuff where it should be, in the past. That sounds amazing to me.

Let's spend the night in the woods again without the phone. Let's spend that night trying to fall in love again. It would be fun to have it around to play with. There is just no explaining it, if we were to get caught with it. The safest bet for us not to be bothered is for this phone to not exist.

Chapter 13: Be the One

We were smoking that joint and I got extremely lethargic and euphoric. That turned into feeling light-headed and dizzy. A thousand things were hitting me at once. They still are.

I'm still trying to wrap my brain around the fact that I possibly get to live the rest of my life here with you. This era was like a fantasy to me growing up. Meanwhile, Jimmy possibly sets a beautiful change in place for all humanity. What a concept to grasp!

You can't understand how special that is to me. The time I grew up in was so intense in a different way. I think mostly because of all the advancements in technology. People lost connection because they spend more time on devices like my phone, which occupies their attention.

Imagine a screen the size of a notebook or a folder. Now, this screen can pull up video, music, and any form of movie, picture or book you want to see. It does this through what I was telling you was called the internet. That's what connects all these devices together.

Think about the post office, you know, how it delivers mail from all over the world. The device gets packages, which are anything from video to audio, entire books from all over the globe just by typing it in and finding it at certain places they call websites or pages. It's difficult to describe these phones and tablets because there's nothing here for me to compare them with.

I'm enjoying my time here without the internet. Instead of everyone messaging you and telling you there's a party at the beach, you just get in your van and drive down there. I love the slower pace of life. I no longer feel like an insignificant ant in an enormous ant hill.

You know how all your friends sit around a fire and actually talk and listen to each other? With all these devices, when people are outside, they just sit around quietly and all mess with their phones in unison. They lost general connection that way. Imagine a whole group of people sitting together all doing things on their phones and devices instead of sharing ideas and thoughts all as a group.

It's good in a way because one person can share these things with a whole group just by finding it on their device. It's bad because people just go into their own world a lot instead of socializing. It's very nice to get comfortable with detachment from the constant over-stimulation. I do not miss all the technology from my day.

All the people are staring at their devices in my time, doing their own different thing. So, therefore no one keeps their full attention to what's going on in the actual room. It's not good. It's not healthy.

I can't wait to lose the energy that comes with those types of random interactions. The scatter-brained attempt at listening we do in my time is not like the calm, conducive sharing you guys do. I really can't really describe it. Everyone is simply stuck in their own zone.

I know it sounds awesome and alien to you, and in a way it is. Every person having their own handheld computer is amazing. It's also a double-edged sword if I've ever seen one.

The way all your friends gather and just be in the moment together is where it's really at. The world's changed in more ways than I could ever possibly tell you, and I'm not sure I would want to. The best thing I can tell you is that I'd rather be here, no question about it.

Some of the changes are obviously bad. Life is so much more satisfying without all that hyperactivity crackling everywhere around us, I promise. It's like people can't sit still. They must have their devices interacting with them constantly.

I'm starting to get used to the calm in the air. It took years, though. I was kind of almost schizophrenic when I first got here. I was so used to my brain computing so many topics at once. It took some getting used to, I mean just being at peace here.

People in my time are so consumed with this fake image they've made for themselves. They represent a life that's sometimes not true on the internet. It's hard to even make sense of. You and your friends live completely in the moment. People in my day are so lost in this persona they want to project.

You guys are really into each other, you're true friends. People in my day are stretched so thin trying to satisfy a hundred people at once it's exhausting, to say the least. Pretty girls have it the worst. They have so many fans it's scary! The way they deal with it is what counts I guess.

It's no different in the way that pretty girls get most of the attention here also. Except, with this internet I'm telling you about there are literally thousands of guys that can contact them constantly. Commitment is really lacking in my day, sweetie. The over-stimulation seems to make it hard to concentrate.

You guys have it made living a life without a bunch of electronic devices chirping every time someone notices them on the internet. That's a fact. My generation has no idea what a life without constant distraction is like. It's hard to find a second's rest in the day I grew up in. The next time you and your friends surf somewhere and relax, and everyone is sitting around a fire talking, just remember what I've told you.

It's impossible, in my time, to find a moment's solstice. I did it though, and I did it with music from your era. That's how I've ended up here. I'm begging you to take me in. If you don't I understand. If you don't it's just the price I have to pay.

I'm hoping my good deeds will help me be in good graces here. I've tried to be a good person up to this point. The universe will guide me through this era, just as it got me here. There's no doubt about that.

I hope you can see it in your heart to truly love me. If you don't, what can I do? Nothing really, but I need you to be the one who shows me around these days. I want you to be the one.

You will be not only my companion and lover but also, tour guide to the West Coast, if I have it my way. I feel like such a tourist. Here is where I wish to stay. It will be with you also, if I'm lucky.

Chapter 14: Life in Limbo

There are going to be parts of your life you are going to absolutely hate. I call these times limbo. Everyone has bad experiences. These days are the hardest.

These are the days you are most susceptible to doing the wrong thing. These are the days when you just need a break or some type of relief almost constantly. Your nerves are the shortest, your spirit is broken or at least damaged during these times usually. You need time to heal.

However, these days are when you are free to do all the things you always wanted to do. You make that movie you want to or write a book. One could become a hippy (given a time machine). This is when you can pick a new path.

You're free to start over and try to create a life closer to what you always wanted or need now. That's what I always try to remind people. The best part of these days in limbo is you're basically forced to reinvent at least part of yourself or your life, if not all of it. It's critical.

I accidentally jumped time first. When I was lying in that

field in 1950s Georgia, I fantasized about coming here. The shock wore off, and I thought about not weaseling back into my old life and starting a completely new one. So now, here we are. The right decision was made. I wouldn't go back to my old life now if I could.

I'm really glad the Glowbox is waterproof because it was flat-out pouring rain when I appeared on that field in the 50`s. I found my way under a tree and did my best to fathom what had happened. It was hard to get my bearings. I felt so disoriented.

I realized I was outside the base, but it was much smaller and seemed outdated. I slowly made my way in. A newspaper lying on a table in the hangar was my source of discovery about where I had ended up. That's the first time the thought of going to a completely different time crossed my mind.

Coming back to my old life didn't sound quite as appealing as vanishing off into the sixties and starting a tie-dye collection. This is what led me right here to you and away from my time was following my heart. I'm having so much fun here. These days are so much better than the 2000's!

When I was an MP, I had more bad days than good ones. Here in the sixties, I have awesome times. With you in my life, sweetie, they are just going to get better, too. You bring a real zing to every day we're together, and you're never boring.

Jumping time suddenly threw me into a rebirth of biblical proportions. I had to start over from scratch with nothing. I had to do it like an outlaw on the run, on top of that. I had to completely recreate myself.

When I first got here, I was starving, broke, and had to become a completely different person. Thank God San Francisco has a decent-sized homeless population. I just blended in with them at first for food and shelter. A homeless illegal immigrant showed me how to get my identification documents and my job.

Bless his heart! Manuel is awesome. He helped work for cash with him. We did concrete work for new construction.

I decided to put a different spin on life than I've ever tried. I wanted to try to be happy. I worried more about what feeling good could feel like than being secure. The Glowbox bringing me here served my needs for this well.

Let's face it: when you're in a place where you must pretend to be someone else, security is out the window. The rug could get swept out from under you at any time. This is not a great feeling, if you've never felt it. Living like that takes paranoia to new levels.

I figured I wanted to come here for a reason. I took that reason to the bank and became the biggest peace-loving hippy I could. According to my cover story, I was just a stoner from Michigan who moved to San Francisco. I never had to talk about the military after that, which was awesome.

It's been good to talk to you about it so, I can get some stuff off my chest. It's nice not talking about it with any else just as much honestly. I don't want to discuss this with anyone else if possible. Let's keep this whole Glowbox thing our dirty little secret please.

Where would you go if you could pick any place in time? It didn't occur to me that I could go anywhere. This was until I had put a great amount of time and thought into sliding back into my old life gracefully. The idea only really rang home about an hour before I used the Glowbox and came here. I rerouted here kind of on a whim after it was charged.

There was an old atlas in the room I was hiding in. That's where I found the coordinates for Warner Robbins. This was when the plan was to go back home. The atlas fell off the box it was on and landed in the bay area. I was joking to myself and thought, "Hey, I could just make my way there and catch some really good shows."

Going back to Georgia and sliding right into my life right before I had to use the Glowbox was the original plan. I changed my mind quite impulsively when I weighed out the options. Your time started sounding way better than mine. I made the right choice.

The Glowbox was charged, and I was hiding up in that storage room in the hangar when I decided disappearing into your time and space just sounded so much n better than my old life. My age is so convoluted and wishy-washy. People are all trapped in their own little bubbles.

I was right too. I do not regret this decision one bit. I have had more fun in my short time here than my whole life leading up to this. That's a fact!

I remember the thought crossing my mind the first time

like a sly dog trying to sneak out some people's food. "You COULD just go to the sixties and catch some rock shows and be a hippy" I thought. The look on my face had to be priceless. I bet I looked like I had just discovered fire.

That's just what I did, though. To be honest, now it all rests on you, Rose. You know all my secrets and you have my heart too. Be easy on me. This guy is completely at your mercy.

I am free of the Glowbox now. Jimmy is off to save humanity. He will or die trying. He's quite prepared for that possibility.

I can truly get lost in this era now and I want to do it with you. I heard the Grateful Dead are playing a free show on the Haight tonight we could go to that and celebrate. That sounds like a good plan to me. How about you?

This is truly a reason to celebrate. The wheels are in motion to wake up to a new world one day. Let's say Jimmy is successful, the entire course of human history could go in a beautiful direction. The thought is so overwhelming.

You may have a hand in changing the way people treat each other for all of eternity. How does that feel? You just thought you were taking some dude to get some pot and ended up saving the world, talk about a wild ride. Guess you never know how things will eventually work out.

If you had the chance to go anywhere in time and space, wouldn't you take it? Would you just stay in your current place? If you had no kids, no serious significant other, and no real attachments, would you take the ride?

Imagine you could go to your favorite time or even some unknown era of the future. That's the choice I had, and I used it. I used to come to the most peaceful, electric place in history I'd ever heard of. It did not disappoint.

Time waits for no man. However, I got to bend the rules, oh and bend them I did. Let's just hope I didn't break something. At least, if I did break something, let's hope it was for the better. I saw my chance and I took it.

I know we got crazy with it, but I hope it goes well. I hope Jimmy saves humanity. I'm just happy to be here with you. There's a whole new mission now, too.

I hope JFK never goes to Texas that weekend. I hope MLK never goes to Memphis. I hope Hitler dies an early death and millions of folks never suffer. Only time will tell.

Let's just say Jimmy does kill Hitler. Does that mean an entire World War won't happen? Just marinade on that for a while. How much different would the human race be if the Nazi party never happened?

Without Hitler's propaganda and global domination schemes, would that World War have still happened? Would millions upon millions of lives be completely different and beautiful? He created awful fates with his power mixed with madness. These are the questions I'm stuck on.

There are terrible forces at work in this world. They will stop at nothing to complete their goals too. What if Jimmy takes the box and sets them back a bit? Good for him. Good for us.

My goal was not to make a huge positive impact on mankind. He is ready to die for that cause! He said if he was shot immediately after killing Hitler then so be it. He meant it too.

Chapter 15: Trippy Jack in a Box

Let me tell you what I know about Jimmy. First off, he`s an army man like me. He did four years before he decided teaching was his strong suit. He said his drill instructors had him showing all the guys how to do almost everything. This way, he knew his role in life was teaching.

The guy really wants to make a difference in the world. That's how he ultimately ended up being a college professor and the new operator of the Glowbox. He learned more a lot the world than anyone would ever need to know. That made him a prime candidate.

He is the definition of a history buff. Jimmy knows everything about different countries and cultures. That's why I truly believe he can kill Hitler. More power to him, too. He already speaks fluent German because he went there in the Army.

It's pure genius how he wants to kill him too. He's going to go back to when he was young and do it then. That way he won't have to deal with the Gestapo and his evil ideas will never have a chance to go public. These things could set in place beautiful changes we can't even fathom.

The plan is to eradicate the entire history of the Nazi party with one move. We called this part Operation Checkmate. The amount of hate that will never be executed and taught is truly hard to fathom. I'm trying to wrap my head around it.

Killing a child sounds savage. However, if you knew it would be the saving grace for so very many men, women, and children, would you do it? Well, he's going to and I'm all for it. How many children will he save by killing one?

The hard part will be charging the Glowbox so he can continue from there. He's going to do it. Jimmy researched the type of power available in Austria back then and created an adapter. He's going to go to JFK first, then Martin Luther King Jr., and then finally, ole Adolf.

I was searching for someone I thought may use the box for the good of all of us. I had almost given up and found Jimmy by pure mistake. There were a couple of ways of trying to destroy and dispose of the Glowbox I was toying with. There was just no way to shake the idea of using it for good, so I didn't.

I first met Jimmy at a party here on the college campus. He was lying in a hammock on this girl's porch talking about history repeating itself. He was going on and on about how society must change bad habits globally as a whole. This way we don't keep falling into the same traps.

I couldn't help but sit down and listen to this intelligent, intuitive rambling. When I left that night, I thought I needed to give the box to someone like him. Then I thought well, why not him? That became my mission.

I started lurking around campus on my time off from work to try and find him again. It didn't take long. I would've searched forever. Giving it away, instead of destroying it, seemed like my only option.

I ran into him at a college bar a couple of weeks later and realized this was my chance. I introduced myself and bought us a round of beers. We talked and shot some pool. I knew this was my moment, so I really tried to make a good impression on him.

I'm not ashamed to say I charmed him a little bit so I could butter him up to take the Glowbox. I am not even ashamed to admit I followed him home. The conversations we had over those pool games made me sure I had found the right one. The man really had conviction about making the world a better place, and I had the tools to help him.

I followed him to a lot of places after that. I truly stalked him. I knew in my gut this was the man to take the time machine. My mission was to become his friend and that's exactly what I did. It wasn't too hard.

That's how I found out he really liked smoking pot. That's also how I found you Rose. So, I really cannot complain about the results of all my sneaky activities. The writing on the wall will teach you a lot if you try to watch for it.

The best way to discuss the Glowbox with him would surely be when he was good and relaxed and/or stoned. I worked my way into coffee with him one day. While we were drinking it, he asked me to smoke a joint with him. While we were in the alley behind the coffee shop smoking it, he said he just wanted to make a good impact on the world. I told him that made two of us.

A lightbulb went off in my head when he said that, and I knew instantly that now was the time to further my interrogation. I said, "If you had a time machine how would use it to make this impact?" he took a big pull of smoke and took it way down, tilted his back, blew the smoke into the sky. He then callously said "I would change the course of evil." Ding Ding Ding! We have a winner folks!

My mission was now clear. Me being an old Army guy meant I was about to give this man the tool to do incredible good or die trying. I had to give this machine another go at things instead of destroying it. The power of the Glowbox is just too great to squander.

This is how you became a part of all this Rose. I'm so glad you did too. Since the mission was successful, we can now disappear into the sixties. We can be happy with the knowledge we may shape the course of human history for a greater good too! Which is heavy.

Sweetie, we can slide back into the beautiful patchwork of love and light as heroes if Jimmy makes good on his goals. He seems like he'll really use it to try to save us all. Let's hope he's successful. Imagine all the things that could be different.

He could also use this great power to do something selfish. I did. Only time will tell. He seemed like was going to try to do what he talked about. Don't you believe so?

He did a lot of preparation after I showed him the machine. He created identification for each of the time periods which will be a big help, I'm sure. To be sure he has money he's taking gold jewelry with him to sell. That's genius.

I took it directly to him after I left your mom's. Hiding my phone and getting the box to him because my top priority after you guys all saw my phone. Honestly, you guys left me completely terrified knowing my secret. Getting those items away from me was the only way I felt peace may be with me.

Months and months of planning my proposal for him to take the machine went straight out the window once you guys had seen the phone. That's why you didn't see me for a week after I got the phone back. Jimmy accepted the Glowbox, and we got to work on his mission. The whole time you were always on my mind, I knew you would love this.

I couldn't wait to get that thing out of my possession and try to get back to running around with you. You see I couldn't even wait that long. I'm glad you got to see him jump time. Are you?

His success became our mission once I had shown him the device. We teamed up on how to pull this off. We truly did a huge amount of brainstorming. No amount of planning can ever completely cover possible dilemmas, but you can be ready for them when they come.

My knowledge of how the Glowbox works will put him off to a good start. He won't be bumbling through time and space like I did. You can charge it on normal plugins, thank goodness. We made a solid game plan.

I'm glad you can charge it, because if not I would've been stuck back in 1950s Georgia permanently. Jumping to a time before electricity would've meant I was stuck! I could've had to live out the rest of my days with the dinosaurs if I had accidentally gone back that far. I was lucky.

He created his own adapter to make it work in 1890's Austria. That way he can get back home after he's done with Adolf, but will he? I didn't. I came here.

You can't blame him if he doesn't. The power to go wherever you want, not to mention, whenever you want is alluring. Having the ability to choose a time and place is pretty intoxicating. The mind begins to get lost in possibilities.

The Glowbox is like a trippy Jack in the box. You've seen it. It literally looks like a metal Jack in a Box with a bunch of glowing numbers and letters. Who could imagine so much energy coming out of something that small?

Have you heard big things come in small packages? Is that even a saying yet? Jimmy being successful in even just one mission could reshape human history. Completing all three could make changes beyond comprehension.

He's gone. Let's go watch the Grateful Dead take over

Haight Street tonight and celebrate. The free show tonight they play in this truck is legendary. Trust me, I have a little insider info, you know I do.

I don't even want to think about this kind of stuff for a night. Let's disappear into the tie-dye and loving energy. I'm so excited. I know, for a fact, this is going to be a great show!

About The Author

CB was born in the foothills of the Appalachian Mountains. Accolades received during college and high school for writing left him with a longing for storytelling. He spent the next twenty years in the big city, finding a culture of people still clinging to the sixties and seventies peace and love era fargone, but not forgotten. This is how Glowbox was born and what led us to this moment. ENJOY!